PLANET LOVE
(The End of the World as We Knew It)

GIANT STEPS PRESS

Advance Praise for Planet Love

If you have ever wondered whether there may be more to the miracle of human life on this planet than what you can now observe, you need to read *Planet Love*.

---David Anderson, author of Q *Will Human Species Survive*

With refreshing candor, infectious wit and a cosmic sense of humor, John Rullo convinces religion and science to embrace, suggesting that what the prophets of old saw may not necessarily be what today's Sunday morning preachers claim. A tale that disturbs and consoles, saddens and exhilarates, *Planet Love* make us more uncertain but more human in the process.

---Reverend Fred Neal

As the world turns apocalyptic, John Rullo experiences an encounter with a spiritual entity that turns his life inside out unfolding a string of events that leads to the end of the world as he knew it as well as his new role in Earth's rebirth. *Planet Love's* story of hope, intrigue and mystery celebrates our human unity with all life and speaks to our everlasting search for the ground of our being.

---Michael Green, author of *Nutrition for the Soul*

In the same way that Rullo's first book, *Blind Spots*, made me re-think attitudes ingrained into my being, *Planet Love* awakened my ability to imagine other forms of reality. The ending's so powerful, I wonder if life as we know it isn't merely illusion.

---Robert Woods

John Rullo addresses religious indoctrination by tactfully alerting us that there's more to the spirit than meets the eye. His *Planet Love* delivers a much needed wake-up call to a world gone way off course.

---Karen Stapleton, East Hampton Wellness Center

Planet Love opened up a longing in me. I had recurring dreams of being part of Rullo's future world where peace, love and understanding finally and genuinely rule.

---Eric Foley, *American Avatar*

If only everyone saw the world through John Rullo's eyes! *Planet Love* exemplifies the liberating truth that to live to the fullest one must live not from the mind but from the heart.

---Ronnie Gavarian, *Gold Coast Review*

ISBN-13: 978-0-61547-580-6
Library of Congress Control Number: 0615475809

Cover design by Rusty Shackleford
Back cover photo by Gerard Comito

Printed in the United States of America

Giant Steps Press
P.O. Box 7539
Freeport, NY 11520
www.giantstepspress.com

Great big heartfelt thanks to my faithful buddies, Maxine Schiller Wilcken and Carolyn Bunkley, for acting as my second & third pair of eyes and catching the many things I missed!

Contents

Allow Me To Introduce Myself

~ PART ONE ~

~ PART TWO ~

I'M LOOKING FOR A PLANET WHERE I CAN GO TO LIVE
WHERE THE PEOPLE ALL ARE LOVING AND QUICK TO FORGIVE
A PLACE WITH NO DIVIDING LINES, NO FENCES GATES OR WALLS
ALL WORKING CLOSE TOGETHER, ALL FOR ONE AND ONE FOR ALL

I'M LOOKING FOR A PLANET WHERE ALL MEN SPEAK THE TRUTH
WHERE PEOPLE LIVE IN HARMONY THE OLD FOLKS AND THE YOUTH
WHERE COLORS BLEND TOGETHER JUST LIKE RAINBOWS IN THE SKY
AND NATURAL CAUSES ARE THE ONLY WAY THAT PEOPLE DIE

CHORUS: I'M LOOKING FOR PLANET LOVE
IT'S GOT TO BE OUT THERE SOMEWHERE

I'M LOOKING FOR A PLANET WHERE THEY DON'T MAKE BOMBS AND GUNS
WHERE CHILDREN HAVE TO BE CONCERNED WITH ONLY HAVING FUN
WHERE THERE'S NO NEED FOR LOCKS AND CHAINS AND BOLTS ON EVERY
DOOR
WHERE EVERYBODY DOES HIS SHARE AND HAPPY TO DO SOME MORE

I'M LOOKING FOR A PLANET WHERE PEACE AND FREEDOM REIGN
WHERE LIVING LIFE IS SIMPLE AND IT'S RARE SOMEONE COMPLAINS
WHERE THERE'S NO SUCH THING AS HUNGER AND THERE IS NEVER NEED TO
FEAR
I'LL NEVER FIGURE OUT JUST WHY WE CAN'T LIVE LIKE THAT HERE

(John Domenic Rullo 2001)
(Recorded by The Cocktails 2009)

~THE END~

~ALLOW ME TO INTRODUCE MYSELF~

Never in my wildest dreams did I think I'd ever be telling the story I'm about to tell. No matter what crazy thoughts I may have entertained during my half-century of life on Earth, none of them could compare to the events that literally turned my days completely upside down. This is an account of those out-of-the-ordinary events leading to this moment in time. As I gaze out upon all this untouched magnificent beauty and splendor, it is my heartfelt desire that my story will be passed along to future generations in hope that man will heed its warnings, embrace its truths and finally attain his full potential.

I think I'm being fairly honest when I say that I'd always been the kind of guy who looked for the good in everyone. For most of my young adult life I never took many things too seriously. As far as I was concerned, life was all about rock 'n roll, making friends and having fun. I strongly sensed that a Divine Entity was responsible for life as I knew it, and somehow, in some way, felt a connection to that Entity. I'd always had a deep love for music and a passion for writing songs. I couldn't agree more to the words of a song by one of my favorite rock groups, The Band, when they sang, "Life is a Carnival." I simply adored it; life, that is, not the song, although it was a really great tune. I was blessed with wonderful parents, relatives, friends and most importantly, a sense of wonder, topped by a sense of humor. I absolutely loved life!

As I got older, just like practically every other guy on the planet, I met a woman, fell in love, raised a family, held down a job, lived paycheck to paycheck and forfeited some of my dreams. Call it surrendering, call it going with the program, but as it is with most decisions, it seemed like a good idea at the time. I had no regrets and held no resentments. I made my own life and for the most part, it was a pretty good one.

During the first few years of our life together, my wife and I were completely out of our mind crazy about each other. Responsibilities were next to nil and we rarely disagreed about anything. Issues of faith and religion were the furthest things from our minds. So elated just to be alive and madly in love, every new day brought along with it yet another reason to celebrate and be grateful. We lived every minute as if there were no tomorrow, never giving too much thought to anything beyond the temporary feel-good thrills of fun and amusement. Time, however, waits for no one, and as hard as I may have tried to keep the hands of the clock from ticking, the years mercilessly pressed on, prompting us to make the joint decision to have children. We had two, Samantha and Daniel. When I became a father, I finally found something I loved more than life itself…my kids.

Unlike a lot of people, and quite contrary to what I believed was my true self, the older I became, the more and more I started thinking about the things that really had no answers, only theories. Sometimes I could feel my body actually tremble as my thoughts would spiral deeper and deeper. I would look into the mirror, touch my face and stare as intensely as I could into my very own eyes. Questions like, "Who am I, what am I, why am I here and where am I going?" would plague me. I became so painfully aware that no matter how those questions were answered, all roads would eventually lead, not only to my ultimate demise, but to my children's. Everybody dies. Not much of an epiphany, I know, still the same, when my thoughts wandered off into the unknown, I became overwhelmed. In spite of the religious indoctrination I received from my parents and my schooling, I wasn't quite convinced about the joys of Heaven and the tears of Hell, which left me basically indecisive about what lay ahead.

Throughout my carefree and reckless high school and college years, I became indifferent about my religious upbringing. The lessons I was taught about Heaven, Adam and Eve and Jesus and Mary, were at one time very comforting bedtime stories, but had no relevance in my frivolous youth. No different than the immortal mindset of most of my generation, I never paid much attention to anything other than grabbing life by the balls and living it to the fullest. I figured when my time eventually comes, which to me was going to be so far off into the future, light years for that matter, assuming there really was such a place as Heaven, I would be there with all my deceased friends and relatives where the partying would continue! If there wasn't, so what! As an aging father, however, with an overactive imagination and a continuous onslaught of bottomless thoughts, I veered back into religion to find answers. For a brief period, my wife and I found vacillating comfort in Bible-based evangelical Christianity. While she comfortably remained inside the box of Born Again Pentecostalism, an internal arousing led me to dabble in various other spiritual belief systems, including Judaic and Eastern religions. Somehow, I was discerning enough to embrace what I saw fit, and to leave behind what jilted my spirit. What stayed with me, however, was the clear and simple truth that all paths eventually led to the same place. What also struck me was that along the way, as long as I trusted my heart and soul, I would never travel alone, a much different concept than the one my spouse chose to cling to. It began to truly frustrate me, seeing the woman I loved so deeply attached to the same doctrine I was overjoyed to break free from. Our taking separate paths at this fork in the road had created a gap in our relationship that just seemed to grow wider. It's funny how unexpectedly change can suddenly creep into one's life, and it's funnier still how someone can expect friends and loved ones to instantly jump on board just because of a sudden revelation. That was a big part of our problem. I expected her to miraculously see through my eyes.

One day while I was in my early 50s, something indescribable, which I will inadequately attempt to describe, happened to me. I was tossing and turning in bed, unable to sleep. My wife was lying fast asleep beside me and I was feeling bad, or perhaps guilty, that we were no longer able to see eye to eye spiritually. The differences in our views had begun to trigger quite a bit of all-consuming marital tension, causing me to occasionally wrestle with my own conscience. Was I right, was I wrong, was I crazy, or did it even matter? Suddenly, on that memorable evening, it was as if strong invisible arms reached out from another realm and actually held me down, causing my complete immobility. While one hand pressed firmly on my shoulder, the other one broke through the thick of my skull, reached deep down into the recesses of my mind and thoroughly removed all the religious clutter that for years had clouded my thinking and hindered my spiritual growth, thus bringing about those unnerving feelings of guilt and unrest. Upon waking the following morning, I was pleasantly stirred and not quite sure if what occurred was just a dream. Dream or no dream, the sensation I had was incredibly liberating. I felt so free and peaceful and encountered the simple but beautiful realization that Love is the guiding force of the Universe, every present moment is a manifestation of Love, and life is a continuous journey to understand and be consumed by that Love. Looking over at the woman with whom

I vowed to remain faithful still sleeping soundly, I realized momentarily, how unfair it was of me to have expected her to surrender her convictions and instantaneously be part of my spiritual journey. There are some roads in life we all have to travel alone. Little did I know, whatever I had just undergone was only a necessary prelude to what was about to happen. Had all of my seeking paid off? Somehow, I felt as though my purpose had been delivered and it was to spread that message of Love and unity to each and every soul I possibly could. I reckoned there had to be some truth in the expression, "Ask and it shall be given." What I imagined my purpose to be, however, was a far cry from what it turned out to be. The story I'm about to tell takes my amazing revelation even a step further. It was the end of the world as I knew it.

****

~ PART ONE ~

****

~ I SWEAR I WASN'T DRINKING ~

It all began on a cold winter's night. On the whole, I have to say it appeared to be a pretty good evening. In spite of the frigid temperature, the die-hard jammers and wannabe singer/songwriters all showed up anxious to perform, making the crowd much better than we had expected. That's just the way it was with Open-Mic nights, feast or famine. On some nights, so many musicians had signed up to perform we couldn't seem to get out of the place by 1AM. On other nights, the turnout was so light that the three of us stood around staring at each other and the ever-so-slow-moving-clock, wondering what songs to play for the few barflies who never seemed to want to go home.

I loved playing with "The Cocktails." Bob, Mick and I were well into our fifties. Each of us had been playing rock 'n roll music since our early teens and the chemistry we had together made us not only sound great, but helped to create an atmosphere of fun. We didn't really take ourselves too seriously. We were well aware that our chances of being rock stars were long gone and we were happy just to have a steady gig. The craziest thing was that we were still covering the same great songs we were playing over forty years ago. I guess part of the reason we were such a good

Open-Mic house band was because of all our experience and the vast amount of songs we knew.

I met Mick quite a few years ago when I sat in as the replacement drummer for the band he was playing with. Somehow we just hit it off and when I asked him if he wanted to join "The Cocktails" and host an Open-Mic with me, he jumped at the opportunity. He was one of the sweetest, interesting and talented human beings I'd ever known. An extremely gifted guitarist, Mick was also very capable at singing and playing various instruments. Whenever he performed, his thinning hair was poorly dyed and sprayed into place, making him appear more like a mad scientist than a rock musician. Pleasantly eccentric and extremely funny, Mick had definitely become an added joy to my life. One evening as the two of us were travelling together on the way to a gig, we were discussing several of those unanswerable subjects, such as, the existence of God and life after death. Mick matter-of-factly dropped the question, "John, do you believe in extra-terrestrial beings?" He then told me he'd been a sky-watcher for at least thirty years and maintained that he'd witnessed several sightings. His interest in UFO's and his explicitly detailed "sighting stories" were quite fascinating but it wasn't until the night I'm about to mention, the night that positively threw my life into a tailspin, when I became certain that whatever claims Mick had made about spaceships were by no means figments of his imagination.

It was Thursday, December 10, 2009. Big Vinnie ended his three-song set with a ripping rendition of "All Along the Watchtower." Watching him try to stretch his chubby fingers along the neck of his vintage Fender Stratocaster, one could tell that he took his guitar playing very seriously. Vinnie would come back week after week because he loved having "The Cocktails" as his back-up band. We had a way of making everybody sound and feel like a rock star. We took him back to his glory days when he was much slimmer, had a full head of hair and was playing lead guitar in local rock bands, wowing the girls with his slick licks and Italian smile. "Man, I got to get myself into a band," he whined in frustration weekly, "I love this shit!"

Vinnie usually stuck around until all of our gear was packed up and loaded into our cars. Once in a while he would lend a hand in carrying a guitar or microphone stand, but for the most part he followed us to and from our vehicles and talked. The truth be told, he was so out of shape, any unnecessary heavy lifting might have proved fatal. Whether he was commenting on the hot looking girl who happened to be in the bar that evening or discussing the specs on his favorite guitar, Vinnie didn't leave until the last of us had started up his car and was on the way home.

I wrapped my scarf securely around my neck, zipped up my parka and put on my gloves, knowing the face-cracking winter cold was waiting outside. I was the first one of "The Cocktails" to have braved it out into the frozen first hours of morning. My car sat alone at the far end of the club's large parking lot, but after hauling drums, amplifiers, guitars and PA equipment to the exit doors, I didn't have the energy to run. My ears were still ringing with the high-pitched howls of electric guitars, the cracking of drums and the rumbling boom of basses, as I nonchalantly walked towards my car, clicking the remote to open the driver's side door. What happened next caused me to stand temporarily paralyzed, frozen in my tracks, and it had nothing to do with the arctic temperatures or the wind chill.

~ CHECKING IN ~

I considered myself pretty fortunate to have retired from the working world at the age of fifty-five. I guess that's one of the things I timed right in my life. I began my career at age thirty, put in my twenty-five years, and with the few good years still left in me, I got to do the things I loved to do like playing in a rock 'n roll band. I kept in touch with my old working buddies and made it a point to see them regularly. With Christmas only a week away, I thought it would have been a suitable time to meet up with the old crew for lunch. Driving for UPS was a bitch on a regular day, but during the Christmas season, no words describe it better than "unrelenting misery!"

UPS guys had all been conditioned to be at the same place at the same time on every working day. I knew with absolute certainty that every Friday at exactly 2PM, six brown trucks would be parked along Manorhaven Boulevard directly in front of Angelina's Pizzeria. Friday December 18th was no different.

Nothing's changed in the two years I'd been away from the job…one large spinach pie, one large sausage pie and a liter of Pepsi. Hanging out with all my work buddies every now and then, even if it was only for the hour while they took time out for lunch, reaffirmed my belief that retiring when I did was a good move. "Johnny," Anthony reassured me after releasing one of the most musical farts I'd ever heard, "You got out just in time, you won't believe how fuckin' bad this job's become!" For as long as I'd known Anthony he'd been taking medication for a troubled colon of some kind. He's one of the few guys I knew who could make his ass sing.

Chuck was always the last one to show up for lunch and living up to his standards, he was late again that afternoon. Crazy Chuck snuck up behind me, threw his arms around me and affectionately cried out, "I miss you Johnny baby! I love you man, great to see you! How are Jillian and the kids?"

"Everyone's good Chuck," I assured him, "Everyone's good!"

He was the only human I'd ever met who could devour an overstuffed Italian hero in milliseconds then fall soundly asleep without batting an eyelash. After hanging with him at lunch every day for several years, something told me that Chuck had been burning the candle at both ends.

"You know I still think about some of the things we used to talk about," Chuck reminisced, then with an almost infiltrating gleam in his eye he continued, "When I wasn't sleeping we used to have many intense conversations! You used to keep it interesting, my friend!"

"I don't know how you put up with me," I humbly admitted, "I was such a hard-head!"

"I loved you anyway, Johnny and I fuckin' miss you man!"

"We all live and learn," I resumed, "We all live and learn…"

Chuck laughed and then reminded me of how at one time I was always trying to shove Jesus down his throat and within a few years how I did a complete turnaround and began ranting about my disdain for religion. "Hey John, you'd go crazy on me anytime I told you I believed there was life on other planets in other galaxies. You'd start quoting the fuckin' Bible and telling me all this shit about God…you were so God-damned opinionated it used to drive me fuckin' nutty!"

"Well Chuck, let's just say I've become a little bit more open-minded!" I replied apologetically.

For the remainder of the Friday lunch hour our conversations touched on the usual topics; current events, work, family and my retirement. I had always been one to try and spark up our discussions with controversial or out-of-the-ordinary subject matter, so without revealing all the spectacular details, I decided to make our chatter a little more interesting.

"Hey guys," I said almost matter-of-factly, "Guess what I saw last week?"

"Oh, here we go!" Anthony chimed in, "What did you see, a naked girl sitting on my face?"

Everybody chuckled as one of my old cronies replied, "You wish fart-boy!"

"What did you see, John?" Chucky asked curiously.

"I know you're going to think I'm nuts, but here it goes…I saw what was unquestioningly a UFO!"

"What the fuck were you smoking?" Anthony asked jokingly as the others laughed along.

"I'm not kidding guys!" I replied, as if I were begging them to believe me, "This time I'm serious…it was incredible…"

"What the fuck do you think I've been talking about all these years?" Chuck shouted with the excitement of a kid at the circus.

"Ah, you're both crazy," the rest of the guys chimed in simultaneously.

Not really sure if they should take Chuck and me seriously, and after some initial ribbing, the conversation matured into an interesting forum on the possibility that UFO's do exist. Suddenly everyone had a different story to tell about a friend of a friend or long lost relative who had made a claim about seeing an unidentified flying object. Pete enthusiastically brought up the Discovery Channel and a series they ran about Roswell and the crop circles. "After seeing that program," he admitted, "There's more reason to doubt that they don't exist!"

Before we knew it, the hour was over, nothing was settled, and all the guys, after wishing me farewell, got back into their trucks and off to their routes. On my way home I thought about Chuck and how I never even considered taking anything he had to say seriously during most of the years we worked together. I never realized how stubborn and tightly shut my mind had become due to the influence religion had on me. I figured, just like practically everybody else, I wanted to be on the winning team.

Later that evening, while I was struggling to stay awake for Letterman's Top Ten, the vibration of my cell phone snapped me out of my late-night trance. "Hello, Johnny," a familiar voice spoke, "It's Chuck. We have to talk."

~THE NEIGHBORS~

"Hey Dad, shut the door behind me, I'm running late," my twenty-five year old daughter Samantha requested in her usual demanding tone as I watched her scurry out of the house and off to work. Sam was always frenzied, an on-the-go kid trying to fit work, graduate school, boyfriend and social life into a seven-day week, so that she hardly had the time to say "Good Morning" and "Good Night." How was I going to throw a wrench into her very calculated busy routine by telling her I saw a flying saucer? Samantha didn't need anything else to think about and confuse her more than she already was.

Looking out from my front door, I saw the daily crumbled up McDonald's wrappers trapped underneath our bushes that had blown over from our next door neighbor's uncovered trash. It wasn't that I was annoyed so much by having to clean up my front lawn because of their inconsideration; I was upset over the fact so many people actually ate that crap on a daily basis. Lena, our neighbor directly across the street, was spreading salt upon her icy front steps as she smiled and waved good morning to Sam. It was trash day so garbage pails lined our street like frozen wooden soldiers awaiting the morning pick-up. Mr. Gambaro, who lived to the right of Lena, was already out his front door. The first thing he would do before taking his brisk morning walk was to check if the garbage had been picked up by feeling the weight of his pails. It had been at least ten years since he had a work-related accident when chemicals splashed into his eyes leaving him virtually blind. We could have set our clocks according to Mr. G's daily walks. He was always a pretty active, hard-working guy. Losing his sight had to suck. I often wondered what kept him going. I'd always try to strike up a conversation with Mr. G at some point in the day just to help him kill some time.

"John-a, is that-a you?" he'd ask as I approached.

"Yeah, Mr. G," I'd answer, "It's me."

"You think it's-a gonna snow-a?" he'd ask me time and time again.

"I think so, they're talking snow!"

"Sum-of-a-bitch-a!" he'd reply every time.

We'd been living in our home for almost twenty years and I still didn't know the name of the woman who resided in the house adjacent to the Gambaro's. Sometimes she would wave if we made eye contact, but for the most part she would just come and go making little or no effort to associate with any of the neighbors. On that particular morning as I watched Samantha pull away from the house, the nameless neighbor smiled and waved to me before turning away to re-hang the Christmas lights that had fallen from her miniature Japanese maple. For over nineteen years we had referred to her as the "lady in the house with the red shutters."

The menorah was still aglow in Lena's window. The morning sun was glistening on the snow-covered lawns, and in timely fashion each of the neighbors headed off to work, school or wherever it was they would go on weekdays. I shut my front door, turned up the thermostat, made my way into the kitchen and put up a pot of coffee. Everybody seemed so content to be going through their monotonous daily routines. I wanted to shake them up so badly, to let them in on my secret that "We're not alone!" At the same time, however, I thought, "Why upset things?" They'd probably just humor me, then behind my back say that I was nuts. Besides, if I was correct in following my instincts, I would have known without any uncertainty when and to whom I could divulge the depths of what I had seen. I took my morning coffee along with me into the den, sat behind my computer and spent hours surfing the Internet, investigating the possibility there may have been others who have witnessed what I had witnessed. I came up empty-handed.

~TORTUROUS~

Christmas was especially grueling for me. As I mentioned previously, a few years before the incident in the parking lot, in what I claim was a supernatural moment, I underwent the most amazing departure from all of my religious indoctrination. In that life-changing instant, all of my spiritual turmoil was settled and religions and their traditions no longer made the least bit of sense to me. It then became increasingly harder and harder to tolerate the insanity of the holiday season. Although I considered myself fortunate to have been somewhat enlightened, I was still very much human and occasionally needed to remind myself to be patient with others. In order to keep peace with my wife and family, with just a little resistance and against whatever convictions I had, I usually submitted to the nonsense and went along with the program. I understood how strange it must have been for them to see such a drastic change in me, but at the same time, I could never go back to wholeheartedly join in on all the festivities. How does one go about trying to explain his or her supernatural encounters without expecting to be thought of as crazy? That particular year it was worse than ever.

I was once again the non-confrontational enabler. In an effort to keep the peace, I found myself standing in a mile-long line at the post office waiting to purchase Christmas stamps. Knowing I was about to spend fifty dollars on holiday-designed postage did not make me very happy. The fact that I was standing in line behind a woman who was repeatedly sneezing without covering her mouth and reeking of a scent so foul it was beyond description was making me even unhappier. The last thing I needed was to get sick. The band had some upcoming holiday gigs and they would have killed me if I got suddenly laid up with the flu. As much as I squawked about not sending out Christmas cards, there I stood resenting every torturous minute.

My eyes slowly surveyed the increasingly growing line and I was oddly amused by the annoyed looks on the faces of all the harried patrons as they impatiently waited to ship out their Christmas presents to distant friends and relatives. As the line slowly advanced, those with the oversized boxes would push them along and, more times than not, couldn't avoid bumping into the persons in front of them, which resulted in an exchange of dirty looks and annoyed mumbling. The heat in the post office was cranked so high that in order to avoid fainting, some folks removed their winter-wear and clumsily tried to hold their coats along with their packages together in their arms. There were no signs of Christmas Spirit anywhere, just fatigued and forlorn faces expressing their yuletide dissatisfaction. All I could think about was how insane an ordeal the holiday frenzy was and how it could have so easily been avoided. It seemed that year after year, more and more people became fed up with the pressure and the needless stress of the tradition's expectations, yet very few have been audacious enough to put their foot down and insist, "We've had enough! We're not going to take it anymore!" Normally my blood would have been boiling and I would have been cursing up a storm in a situation such as the one I was in, but ever since the revelations, nothing seemed catastrophic enough to get overly upset over. If there was one thing I learned from both of my eye-opening experiences, it was to try to approach all things with patience and love in spite of my opposition to them.

Although at that point I knew more than ever how completely pointless and ludicrous many of our traditions were, in obedience to what I believed was the prodding from a higher intelligence, I knew I just had to hold my tongue and bide my time. Once again, I endured the madness of another Christmas season, viewing the religious no differently than those with mental disorders.

~WAKE ME SHAKE ME~

When I saw the caller-ID flashing Ross's name and number, I was pleasantly surprised. Ross and I used to play together in the same band during the late 70's, early 80's. I hadn't seen him in a few years and although we made it a point to call one another periodically, it had been a while. "John," Ross's gravelly voice spoke out in an unusually somber tone, "Sorry, man, but I've got some bad news to tell you…"

"What's up, Ross?" I asked curiously, wondering what depressing information he could have possibly had to pass on to me. I was aware of his Mom being ill, but for some reason, I also knew it had to be something other than an update on his mother's health.

Ross coughed to clear his throat and resumed, "Jeffrey's wife died!"

Ross had introduced me to Jeffrey right after my band had lost our bass player. We were just about to go into the studio to record some demos and needed a replacement immediately. Jeffrey stepped in and did an incredible job. Since then we'd played together on various projects, and through Ross, we had kept up on each other's lives.

From my dealings with Jeffrey, I'd always found him to be a rough-around- the-edges kind of guy, yet pleasant enough to play with and be around. I knew his wife had been sick for quite a few years and Jeffrey devoted himself to taking care of her, thus sacrificing much of his life and what he loved to do, which was playing music. I was sorry to hear of her death, especially at such a young age. Death, however, was part of life and sooner or later every last one of us was going to have to cash in our ticket out of here.

Ross also informed me of Jeffrey's request to ask all of his artistic cronies, namely musicians, writers and the like, that if they planned on coming to the funeral parlor to pay their respects, to please do so on the last night of the viewing. Besides wanting to offer my condolences, I thought it would be cool to see many of the musicians I'd crossed paths with through the years.

As I entered through the front door of the funeral home, Jeffrey spotted me right away and came over to greet me. We shook hands, hugged and I told him how sorry I was to hear the news. He thanked me for coming and led me back into the room full of old familiar faces. It was certainly nice seeing everyone and catching up on the events of their lives. It was somewhat agonizing to be among so much gracefully aging, amazing talent and realize not a single one of us hit the "big time." Everyone seemed genuinely happy to see one another and be able to rehash all our "battle stories" of the trials and tribulations of the music business and recall how we were all at one time "almost famous."

Suddenly, Jeffrey's deep commanding voice rose above the drone of all the creative visitors, directing us to kindly take a seat. Although the slight vibrato in his speech made it easy to detect his nervousness, I, for one, had no idea of what was to follow. Clearing his throat and taking several deep breaths, Jeffrey began to explain the religious epiphany he had which enabled him to care for his ailing wife for so many years. "A wife is not supposed to die before her husband," he ranted passionately, "A husband's duty is to protect his wife; I'm a poor excuse of a man, and

I failed in taking care of my beloved spouse!" His perspective didn't make the least bit of sense to me, and though I thought he was being way too hard on himself, I listened politely as he "enlightened" the small but attentive crowd that he and his deceased wife did not believe in the conventional God of most religions. They chose to worship the Feminine Divine, a creative entity he addressed as Goddess. In their world, it was evident that women were held in much higher regard than men. At that moment, it kicked in as to why the entire funeral parlor was adorned with pictures and statuettes of female angels.

Jeffrey handed out photocopies of a prayer and a hymn he had written to this Goddess and asked if we would please oblige him by singing along. All heads were looking down at the words to Jeffrey's unorthodox style of worship, eyeballs stretching to the far corners to see if everybody else was joining in. "Sing you bastards, sing!" he cried out, as he clutched the hand of his wife's lifeless corpse. Everybody politely, yet reluctantly, followed Jeffrey's lead, singing along but not quite catching on to the melody. We sounded like a choir of mentally challenged crooners. Ross gave me a look, and in that brief glance I knew we were on the same page. Words weren't necessary to convey our mutual feelings that Jeffrey had lost it! It was also at that very moment that I was overcome by a sudden intuitive surge signaling me that Ross was probably someone I should remain in close contact with. I was relatively certain I would soon be sharing with him what I had been keeping bottled up inside me for weeks. I was also absolutely sure, however, that Melinda's wake wasn't the right time to spontaneously bring up any conversation about UFO sightings, but I felt that a meeting in the immediate future between Ross and me to discuss what could very well be our calling was inevitable.

When the bizarre song service came to a close, Jeffrey dismissed the respectful crowd. I wrapped my scarf around my neck, buttoned up my coat and after bidding my farewells to all my old acquaintances, Ross reached out to shake my hand. He pulled me close, gave me a hug and said reassuringly, "We need to get together soon, man! We have a lot of catching up to do!" They say the eyes are the windows to the soul. In that instant, something in Ross's eyes revealed his longing to release many untold tales. Since it was already late and we both had taken in enough strangeness for one night, it just seemed logical to wait until we met again.

As peculiar a tradition I found wakes to be, that one was strangely entertaining. If it had been ten, fifteen years prior, because I didn't know any better, I probably would have politely excused myself and left the service, not wanting to take part in any ritual that was such a far cry from what I professed to believe. I could only imagine how my wife Jillian would have reacted. Finally being able to recognize the absurdity of belief systems and the ways in which people defended them, I felt like the cat that ate the canary. My opinions, however, weren't going to miraculously bring harmony to the room or any comfort to Jeffrey, so I kept them to myself. Why be confrontational and confuse people any more than they already were? Soon enough they were all going to see for themselves…

~BACK TO THE MORNING AFTER~

It was four in the morning by the time I gently crawled into bed on the night of December 10th. I was busting to tell Jillian what I had seen just moments ago, but knew that waking her from a dead sleep wasn't the way to go about telling her something so outlandish. She would not have been at all receptive; besides, it was bad enough we'd already had such differences in what we believed and did not believe. I figured it could've just waited until I awoke the next afternoon.

I lay on my back staring at the ceiling, knowing it would've been next to impossible to fall asleep. "Why me?" I asked myself over and over again, "On a planet occupied by billions of people, why was it that I was singled out and given such a privilege, if what I saw could even be considered a privilege?" Most of my friends and relatives already maintained I was out of my mind and delusional due to my past religious phases; mentioning that I saw something from outer space would have only added fuel to the fire.

Feeling as if I had overdosed on caffeine, with eyes wide-open I lay still and wondered, rethinking everything I'd ever believed. I contemplated the prophets of the Bible. What did Moses really see? Was there really a Moses? What did Jesus really mean when he said ordinary men would be able to perform miracles greater than he did? My mind was swirling with images of ancient Egypt, the Sphinx and the Pyramids. How did who we considered to be "primitive man," construct such complex structures with such precision? Who or what enabled Nostradamus to make his far-reaching predictions? Just how many enlightened messengers have walked the Earth and have tried to awaken humanity to the idea that perhaps we're not alone? Did they see what I saw? Suddenly I was contemplating the plight of the dinosaurs, the evolution of man and the undeniable fact that the Earth had been here for countless millions of years. How could a book which recorded only six thousand years of history be the last word on all that exists? Did I just find my purpose or did my purpose find me? As much as I was confused, I was certain.

I closed my eyes and took several deep breaths in an attempt to relive in my head all I had seen less than two hours ago. But it was so much more than what I beheld…whatever it was I was subjected to, entered my very being…The visions, the thoughts, the information all seemed to meld together and become one with me…How long was I out there? It couldn't have been very long at all or else Mick would have come looking for me. The parking lot was desolate…the sky was clear…the bitter December chill penetrated right to the bone. I remember stretching out my arm and pointing the remote towards my car to unlock the doors…I wasn't looking up. It was right out there, just above the rooftops…a light so huge and so bright, unlike anything I'd ever seen before. I recalled just staring…time seeming to have stopped…and I no longer felt cold.

Under the warm security of my blankets, letting go of my suspicions and my skepticism, I tried not to second-guess myself. I needed to relax. I knew what I had seen and I wanted those revelations to replay in my conscious mind slowly…and they did.

I was transfixed by the immense brightness of the object in the sky until the light seemed to totally envelop me. Ordinarily, light of that intensity would have been blinding, but instead it enhanced my vision, making everything surrounding me glow with crystal clarity. It was as if I were seeing for the very first time.

Waves upon waves of images were streaming into my head like rushing water overflowing a levee. I did not hear any audible voice; it was more like impulses coming from the radiance were permeating my consciousness…I was a vessel for the transfer of information…Matter, energy, the illusion of time, good, evil, life and death…In a solitary moment there was no separation between me and all that existed. I understood what it meant to simply "be"; comprehending all and wanting nothing, like a baby in the warm shelter of a mother's womb.

I wasn't at all frightened, in fact, I felt quite tranquil. Although I was astounded by the vast amount of descriptive data that was passing through my brain, not for a moment did it feel like I was on overload. I craved to know more. Crystal-like fragments the size of snowflakes began to encircle me, moving faster by the second…or was it millisecond? Was time even real at that point? I didn't know. The glimmering and the illumination was overwhelming leaving me almost breathless, weightless… was I seeing God? In a single flash I beheld my own birth followed by fleeting glimpses of everyone who had ever entered my life.

I remembered spiraling helplessly downward and the brightness dimmed until I no longer had any connection to who I was. I seemed to have lost all sense of identity…then suddenly, for a fraction of a split second, there was total blackness, yet keen awareness. I was blind yet I could see. Bursting from out of the blackness, streaking through my mind at a velocity so rapid I couldn't even attempt to explain, came even more detailed images…images so striking, so splendid, so vibrant and magnificent. As in the New Testament story of John on the Island of Patmos, I was being treated to revelations way beyond any man's capacity to understand. I stood motionless and in complete astonishment. A multitude of shimmering explosions, comparable to millions of skyrockets going off in rapid succession, and displays of colorful flares and shooting embers making Grucci's fireworks seem like the spark of a match, culminated with bolts of lightning, giving way to an array of incalculable spinning stars and planets. I was standing before a huge canvas observing the artistic tantrums of a mad painter randomly flinging blobs of rich colors to splatter and ultimately create his masterpiece…the Universe.

In less than a heartbeat, I was transported to a past bountiful Earth where towering redwoods instantaneously sprouted from seed, flowers pulsated with hypnotic rhythms and rushing streams of crystalline water split mountain-like rocks in two. Creatures, both familiar and unfamiliar to me, roamed freely and fearlessly, confident as to their purpose and place in the cosmos. Though I longed so deeply to be part of that scene, my desires were ignored as I was swiftly taken up by swirling iridescent clouds. Above the clouds were square mile sheets of elaborately designed plate glass separating the Earth from the heavens. As I went crashing through it, I could hear it shatter as millions of geometrically designed fragments rained down upon the Earth below me. I was then carried away to a city lined with headstones, where gardens were non-existent and majestic cathedrals, each behind lofty gates made of gold crosses, were lined up one after another. Spiraling silver cylinders sped through the stratosphere, followed by mammoth flames appearing to devour anything and everything in their path. Destruction ensued rebirth…resulting once again in destruction…then rebirth. It seemed to be an eternal pattern where doom only meant hope. There was perfect order to it all… past, present and future were all one moment.

Next thing I knew, in a moment as sudden as the crack of a whip, I heard the sound of a beep as the locks of my car door popped open. Gazing out, I caught the unmistakable sight of a UFO streak above the rooftops. Then, as quickly as it appeared, it vanished into a slit in the sky without leaving a trace. At that point, I was totally bewildered, not sure of anything. I remembered running across the street, from the parking lot back to the club, and from the look on my face, Mick already knew what I was going to say.

"You saw something, didn't you?" Mick snickered, "Tell me all about it!"

Vinnie stood by looking at the excitement in both our faces and feeling a little left out, he muttered, "Hey you guys, what the fuck are you talking about?"

"Flying saucers, Vinnie," I answered, "I'm positive I just saw a fuckin' flying saucer!"

"Huh? You don't believe in that shit, do you?"

"They're out there, Vinnie!" Mick said grinning from ear to ear, "They're out there!"

Vinnie waved his arm through the air and bobbing his head from side to side said, "You guys are fucking with me!"

As if someone hit the pause control, the scene came to an abrupt stop in my mind. I glanced over to see Jillian sleeping so soundly beside me and could still hear the resonance of Vinnie's nervous laughter playing in my head like a soundtrack to a movie. Finally, I turned on my side, facing away from my wife, buried my head into my pillow and drifted off to sleep.

~SEEING IS BELIEVING, I GUESS~

When my eyes slowly opened on the morning of Friday, December 11th, I launched myself out from under my blankets and wondered if all the thoughts dazedly spinning through my mind were the results of a dream. I couldn't believe I was up so early after getting to bed so late and not being able to fall asleep. While rubbing my eyes and shaking my head, everything gradually started to come into focus. I was unquestionably sure I saw what I saw. Somehow, someway, incredible amounts of images, suggestions, theories and perceptions were transmitted into my very essence. How in the world was I going to convince my immediate family-or anyone else for that matter-what I witnessed was real? Real or not, whatever I encountered had become a permanent part of my consciousness. How could I ever go on to look at life the same?

I found my way down the stairs to the kitchen where I made myself a pot of much needed coffee. Jillian was in the den totally engrossed in Rachel Ray's recipe of the day. "John," she asked without even looking up to see the dazzled look in my eyes, "Doesn't this look delicious?" How were my tales of extra-terrestrials, visions and a UFO going to compete with portabella mushroom cacciatore?

"Yeah, that looks scrumptious!" I answered disinterestedly, "but I have something crazy I have to tell you about last night!"

"More wacky performers at Open-Mic night?" she asked.

Although deep within I had an unexplainable confident suspicion that I should not mention a word about what had transpired the night before, how could I not share my latest life-altering news with my wife?

"Jill," I said, ignoring the inner voice, "You're not going to believe what I saw last night!"

With three quarters of her attention on what she was planning to prepare for the night's dinner, she replied, "What, John, what did you see, another ghost?" remembering the night I thought for sure I saw an apparition in our bedroom.

"A freakin' UFO," I answered excitedly, "Big and bright and right there in front of my face! Like nothing I'd ever seen before; it was amazing!"

I was understandingly aware that if one didn't see it for oneself, sharing in my enthusiasm would be quite difficult. I went on to describe to the best of my ability what I saw in the sky, and all Jillian could respond with was, "Oh cool, did you tell Mick?" knowing the UFO enthusiast he was.

For several years, my wife and I hadn't been able to agree on issues of spirituality and religion. She found comfort in attending a local Christian Pentecostal church, whereby I underwent a "coming-out" that had led me down a spiritual path that resisted the doctrine she firmly stood by. How in the world was I going to tell her lights from the firmament allowed me to behold creation, see eternity and for all I know, see God? I decided not to.

"Yeah, Mick was pretty excited!" was all I said. She was content believing that Jesus was coming back to save her and fellow believers from the terrifying wrath of God. When I dared to tell her differently, her self-righteous attitude flew and an argument usually developed. I could only imagine what she would have thought if I told her if Jesus were coming back, he'd be travelling in a space ship. I just left it at that and wandered about the house for the remainder of that afternoon in a stupor.

In what seemed like another lifetime, many years ago, I subjected myself to the fire and brimstone ranting of a Pentecostal pastor who forever warned his conditioned congregation about the fires of Hell and the need to be covered by the blood of Christ in order to avoid spending eternity in gut wrenching, teeth-gnashing torment. He would continually call attention to all the catastrophes occurring in the world indicating "the end is near." For over two thousand years man has been making the very same claim, "Repent!" Fortunately, I was gratefully awakened and able to escape the narrow-minded doctrine of an insane belief system. I wasn't sure if I would ever find what I was looking for, but I was positive it wasn't in the confines of a church or in the pages of an ancient book.

In the short span of just two decades, I had seen technology advance in leaps and bounds. Those advancements, however, brought along with them a bombardment of up-to-the minute news reports, most of them bad. Telecommunications had truly made the world a smaller place. Sometimes I could understand how the "faithful" had been coaxed into believing those Sunday morning "Messengers of Doom" were right. The news media only added to the frenzy with their continual onslaught of tales of terror. I'd always been certain that the natural disasters civilizations had faced through the centuries, such as earthquakes, volcanoes, hurricanes and tsunamis, were nothing more than the natural pangs of a changing Mother Earth. To think these disasters were the revengeful acts of a jealous and angry God always struck me as completely ludicrous. Murder, greed and the many acts of inhumanity that filled the headlines were just results of unconscious human behavior, not the workings of a lurking devil.

Whenever I considered the space-age technology of the early twenty-first century, I wondered how for so many centuries humankind seemed to be at almost a standstill. Why had it taken the human mind such a long span of time to progress from the invention of the wheel to the telephone, and in just the blink of an eye, arrive at the know-how to create the Internet and lightning speed computer processors? Had we been getting assistance from a higher form of intelligence? Were they among us? Have they been here assisting past civilizations? Does humanity keep failing and if so, why? It also perplexed me to know that ever since the day in 1885 when Karl Benz invented the gasoline-powered internal combustion engine, the automobile industry had continued into the 21st century to utilize the same primitive motor to power their vehicles. How could we have been so advanced, yet so archaic? There most definitely had to be a reason why I was given the honor of being exposed to such illuminating visions. With it, however, there had to be great responsibilities. Come hell or high water, I had to figure out what and why.

~THERE'S SOMETHING HAPPENING HERE~

The Eruptions, who had always been one of my favorite local bands, were playing at a neighborhood bar on a Saturday night, so Jill and I along with my bass player Bob and his wife Bern, decided to go and show support. Unless my band was playing, I was never really a fan of hanging out in bars. The place was hopping with a well-over occupancy crowd and the band sounded great as they ripped through a rockin' version of The Doors' "Peace Frog." As we tried to wriggle our way through the swarm of Eruption fans and locals, after what seemed like a few professional ballroom dance steps, we finally made our way up to the bar. Leaning back, Guinness in hand, I gazed out at the crowd, mildly entertained by the weekend mating dance rituals. Watching as women with beer bottles in hand planted their asses firmly in the crotches of their dancing partners, and seeing the men on the verge of instant gratification, was like watching a Nova series on the breeding habits of humans. I thought to myself, "Humans are no different than insects and dogs!" I had become an observer, always conscious of the possibility that at any moment there could be someone I might connect with. I needed to trust that whatever was going to happen was going to happen. Certain things were simply out of my control. I knew I had to re-learn how to just live in the moment, but it became progressively difficult not to think ahead.

As in many crowded pub situations where rock 'n roll and alcohol are prime ingredients, it's only a matter of time before some idiot starts brawling with some other idiot over something insignificant, senseless and downright stupid. At the far corner of the bar, an intentionally obvious biker, stereotypically clad in a well-worn black "Motorhead" tee-shirt and silver-studded leather vest, straddled his barstool, showing the effects of one too many shots of Jagermeister. The oversized key ring dangling to the right of his skull and crossbones belt buckle held more keys than a warden at Riker's. Standing maybe six feet four and weighing at least a solid two hundred seventy five pounds, he suddenly grabbed hold of the arm of a meek sort of fellow in a plum-colored Izod golf shirt who was not even half his size. With the intensity of a battering ram crashing through a castle door, the Harley man pummeled his fist right into the center of the smaller man's gut. Holding his stomach, his face grimacing with agony, the poor guy fell to the ground, spewing vomit all over everyone around him.

"That'll teach ya' motherfucker, don't mess with my fuckin' money!" the rough-neck assailant cried out, foam from his saliva attached to the protruding wiry strands of his uneven beard. Looking as if he were just about to land his worn-out motorcycle boot into the side of the head of the dude on the ground, he snarled as the bar's two hefty bouncers stepped in, and restrained the attacker from doing any further damage. Girls were crying out, "My God, My God!" and right in the middle of the J. Geil's classic, "Love Stinks," the band was ordered to stop playing. Within seconds, six police were on the scene, the bully was hand-cuffed and while trying to shrug off the cops, he continued to salivate while screaming in a WWF tone of voice, "Motherfucker, I'm gonna kill you motherfucker!"

The four of us remained glued to our barstools and watched in amazement at how much blood the sorry fellow on the floor was coughing up. One of the police officers called for an emergency medical team while two others tried as best as they could to comfort him. Bob reached for the twenty dollars he left sitting on the bar and asked me if maybe we should go, but suddenly I was filled with a compelling need to stay. I had to be confident that the semi-conscious man on the floor was going to be alright. It wasn't even a minute or two after that caring thought occurred to me, when a very pretty Asian girl, who could not have been more than twenty, twenty-five years old, came running into the bar. "Daddy!" she sobbed, "Daddy!" and fell to her knees beside him. The young woman then straddled herself above whom I presumed was her father, and placing her hands on his brow, shuddered while seeming to pray intensely over him. As the police tried to pull her away, the wounded man opened his eyes and cried out, "Aja, it's okay, I'll be alright!" Obviously, someone in the bar must have known the man well enough to summon his daughter, or it's anyone's guess how she just happened to show up almost immediately after he was beaten, but sometimes truth is stranger than fiction.

Following right behind her, the EMT's entered the scene and as they carefully placed the young girl's beaten father onto a stretcher, she turned and looked up directly at me. For a very brief moment our glances locked and something unexplainable in her piercing eyes seared into my consciousness. From that instant, I couldn't shake her penetrating stare from my thoughts. As she followed the medical team that carried her father out of the noisy club, with every other step she turned her head to look at me as if she recognized me as someone from her past or future… Amidst all the confusion, my eyes were locked in on her every move until she exited the bar and was out of sight.

It turned out that the innocent victim got the living daylights beat out of him due to an unfortunate case of mistaken identity. The story was reported in a local newspaper later that week. Instead of trying to explain that he had the wrong guy, the frail little man, a local fellow whose name was stated as Benjamin Wilkerson, politely told the biker to "Fuck off!" (Of course, in the paper it read, "He blurted some obscenities..." I have always been dumbfounded about the way humans have become so uptight over the use of certain words.) The article also went on to inform that the daughter's name was Aja, just like the Steely Dan song, and she had been adopted by Ben on one of his many business trips to Korea. Benjamin was hospitalized because of severe bleeding, but doctors guaranteed he would be alright. The biker remained nameless and was released from jail because Mr. Wilkerson did not press charges. Human behavior was making less and less sense to me.

It just so happened that weeks later, the same local paper did a feature on adoption in America and printed an interview with Benjamin. I was at the local convenience store when I caught a glimpse of Aja and Ben on the front page of the Lakeside Ledger and my curiosity led me to buy a copy. It seemed that Mr. Wilkerson was an upstanding citizen who happened to be in the wrong place at the wrong time, and the management at the Ledger, to make amends for the bar brawl story, decided to highlight him in a human interest item. The article was a touching story about a business associate of Ben's who had mentioned to him that he and his wife were considering adopting a child from an orphanage near a factory where they did business. The piece further elaborated how Ben, on one of their visits, had unassumingly joined his friend, never imagining that he too would be filling out adoption forms. Ben's heart broke when he saw all the parent-less children and as soon as his eyes met Aja's, he felt an immediate connection and did whatever was necessary to bring her back home with him to the States. Life presents all of us with many crazy and interesting turns. How one man's visit to an orphanage in Korea would one day affect my life was mind-boggling.

~I DON'T EVEN LIKE FOOTBALL~

For quite a number of years my wife and I had been attending Super Bowl parties at Jimmy's house, the brother of our friend Dean. Due to our lack of interest in football, the running joke among the attendees was the way Dean and I had become known as "The Football Homos." Dean and I would pretend we knew what was going on in the game, mimicking everyone else as they cheered and booed, when all we really cared about was the half-time entertainment, the beer and the hot bodies of the gorgeous cheerleaders.

I was never much of a sports fan, but when it came to the Super Bowl, I didn't have to be. Every year Jimmy's place would be crammed with friends, relatives and with what appeared to be a limitless supply of assorted beer and food. As the years progressed, so did the size and the picture quality of his television. It became the event of the year. His living room was decorated with the appropriate teams' football jerseys hanging from the curtain rods and team helmets sitting upon the mantel like trophies. But what made the day really exciting for everyone was the chance to win big money and prizes in the football pools and boxes. I, who never really got involved in the game's action, actually won the big prize money, not just this once, but another time prior. It was kind of ironic for someone who really wasn't too fond of the sport to be the big winner. One year I remember standing in the kitchen yakking to Dean's sister about a movie we had seen, when Jimmy called out excitedly with three minutes left in the game, "Hey John, if nobody scores, you win the big money!" For the next three minutes I became quite the fan. Eagerly waiting for the seconds to tick away, my heart raced with the anticipation of going home with some extra cash! They did, and I did. It was amazing to me how the chance to win a few dollars caused my body to react so irregularly.

I became quite aware as to what was meant by the expression, "Ignorance is bliss." Would I have been better off looking at life less seriously? Why couldn't I just see the fun in competitive sports, go with the flow and try to enjoy events like the Super Bowl and the World Series? Why was I cursed (or blessed) with the incessant need to seek the unanswerable? Why wasn't it possible for me to have both? In my eyes, the concept of competition at that level was plain foolishness since even the losing team walked away winners, monetarily speaking. The only losers were the fans who gambled and took the games too close to heart. Many diehard devotees actually experienced deep depression for days after their team was defeated.

The volume blaring out of the giant flat-screen was deafening and the artificial excitement, which seemed to be created by the nation's media giants, was indeed baffling. Occasionally I found a seat among the roomful of sports enthusiasts, and with beer in hand, jokingly faked some exhilarated interest. The highlights of this high holyday of sporting events were the TV ads. Corporations spent multiple millions to get their commercials aired during the big game. Madison Avenue ad executives worked round the clock trying to create advertisements that would appeal to the audience by pushing the limits as to what the FCC would allow to be viewed on nationwide television. When my band played the bar scene, it was never about the music or how good the band sounded, it was solely about how much beer was sold. The same held true for televised professional sports. It was all logically (or illogically) connected. Sports, music, politics, Budweiser, sex and religion…everything was linked with one purpose in mind…keep the masses asleep (or at least distracted) and try to make as much blasted money as possible!

Although I wasn't quite sure what was going on in the game, I did know that the commotion in the room was exhausting. As everybody was laughing hysterically over the latest intelligence-insulting Bud ad, I suddenly started feeling claustrophobic and a bit feverish. I was only beginning my second beer of the night so I knew the feeling wasn't coming from overindulgence. Just then, in what I can only describe as a kidnapping of my inner being, I felt as if for a fleeting moment, I had entered another dimension. At first it occurred to me I might have been having an anxiety attack, but then flashbacks from that extraordinary night played through my mind at the most staggering pace as an inaudible voice kept repeating, "Be tolerant, be alert and know there is a purpose…." As abruptly as it took hold, it was gone, and nobody in the room had the slightest inkling as to what had happened. Similar incidents were becoming quite the norm for me; I just never knew when they were going to strike.

It was somewhere in the third quarter when my unnoticed disappearance and secret communication had occurred, and surprisingly, I didn't seem to miss a second of the game. It was another one of those mysterious instances when time stood still. I scanned the room wondering if there was going to be that receptive exchanging glance from anyone, but my investigative gazing came to an abrupt end when my cell phone vibrated. It was a text message from my son Daniel, who had just informed me that he and his girlfriend, Johanna, had just broken up. "I knew this was going to happen," he wrote, "Fuck religion…I'm so upset!"

He had explained to me earlier in the week how he and his partner of four years had discussed their spiritual differences and how she suddenly saw an uncertain future with him. She needed to feel secure in knowing her future husband would accompany her to church and agree on bringing up their children in the Christian faith. I couldn't help but get the uneasy feeling it was my influence that led him to his rebellious spiritual views. I'd always wanted my kids to figure it out for themselves and more often than not I was forcefully outspoken. Daniel had a much broader concept of God than the "Only Jesus Saves" idea tightly embraced by she who had just become his ex-girlfriend.

"Dan," I said consolingly, "It's going to be alright. If you guys were meant to be together, she'll be back…"

"Dad," he answered despondently, "I don't get it. How could she be so fuckin' brainwashed?"

I knew he wasn't quite ready to handle what I yearned to share with him, so I just reassured him that everything was going to work out with or without her. In my heart I had the strongest feeling it was going to be without her. Within the core of my very being there was a continuous vibration alerting me something huge was stirring. Whatever it was, it was going to affect all of mankind and it was going to be soon. I wasn't clear as to how, what, where or when, but I was sadly aware that Daniel's former girlfriend, Jillian and I weren't going to be facing the inevitable future together. How oddly coincidental it seemed that my son was going through the very same frustration of not being able to openly discuss his true feelings about "God" with the one person he was so confident would be his life partner. Just like Jill, her stubbornness against entertaining broader ideas about our existence was baffling and exasperating.

As far as I knew, my daughter Samantha was still on the fence and like her mother, did not care to discuss matters concerning spirituality. Sam said it reminded her too much of dying. She wasn't a fan of church but she thought my way of thinking was too far out. The trouble with Sam was that she didn't have the desire or the interest to search. Maybe she was too preoccupied with dealing with life's little problems or maybe she was scared. Dan had a very open mind and was indeed seeking, but to paraphrase Scripture, "You can't be a prophet in your own home…"

Receiving Dan's text took my mind even further off the game, dampening what little exuberance I had managed to muster up. While I was engaged in sending a reply message to my son, Jill noticed that my attention was not on the game but on my cell phone and asked who it was I was texting. "It's Dan," I said grimacing.

"Is everything alright?" Jill asked with a mother's concern.

"Yeah, just a little girl trouble," I answered despondently, "they'll work it out…"

As I spoke those words, I thought about Jill and me and how for years I kept hoping we would work out our spiritual differences. In the long run, I knew Dan would be better off without Johanna. Eventually an "unequally yoked" relationship would only bring about frustration, misery and heartache. I guess we all have to figure it out for ourselves so why should it be any different for Dan? I must say, however, while I had no answers to help my son, I knew I was going to win the pot that night! In a repeat performance from a previous Super Bowl, Jimmy called out from across the room, "Hey John, if they hold them, you win the big money, my man!" They held them. Somehow money always seemed to show up when I needed it.

~WHAT TOOK YOU SO LONG?~

It was on a Saturday morning in late March when I finally received the long-awaited phone call from Chuck. Ever since he called me on that night back in December, I had been expecting to hear from him and assumed it would have been a lot sooner, but everything was timing, I guess.

"Hey Johnny," he addressed me in a chipper tone of voice, "It's Chuck, are you busy today? I was thinking we could meet for a cup of coffee or something and catch up on things."

"Chuck!" I happily retorted, "Looking forward to it…name the time and place!"

A few hours later, Chuck and I were sitting face to face at the Lakeside Diner over what were endless refills of black coffee. Chuck was all smiles and extremely fidgety, looking as if he were busting with things to say.

"Johnny," he whispered, in a manner very much like a top secret government spy, "I know you saw something spectacular, man, and I'd been waiting a long time to talk to someone about this! The day you showed up and met the guys for lunch, I was so full of vibes coming from you man, and after the things you said to me…I just fuckin' knew man, I knew it was you." Chuck was so energized it appeared as though he was high on amphetamines. Very much like a rambunctious child unable to sit still, he twitched and twisted, nervously stirring his coffee until he finally leaned across the table. When his bubbling face was just inches from mine, he said in an animated sort of way, "Wasn't it fuckin' awesome? Puts a whole new perspective on life, my friend, doesn't it?"

As we were conversing and trying to figure out the strange phenomenon that had become part of our lives, Chuck was doodling away on his place mat with a number two pencil. After about fifteen minutes of shading and erasing, he grabbed hold of the place mat and dropped it down facing me. "Look familiar?" he asked anxiously awaiting a reaction.

Never realizing Chuck was such a talented artist, I stared at the drawing with jaw-dropping astonishment. Slamming my hand down onto the table, I quivered excitedly, "My God Chuck! That's it exactly!" Chuck's sketch was a perfect representation of what I saw in the sky on that night three months prior. I reached across the table, grabbed Chuck's arm at the wrist and initially uncertain as to what his answer would be, I asked with hopes of hearing what I needed to hear, "What else happened, Chuck? What else did you see?"

Chuck seemed a little bit confused and said, "What do you mean, what else did I see? I saw a fuckin' UFO, man! What else was I supposed to see, little green men?" His eyes were gleaming and his words weren't able to get out of his mouth fast enough, sort of like a crowd of people pushing and shoving at the exit doors of a sold-out theater. "Johnny, it was, uh, I mean, no one would believe it, man, you saw it! It was fuckin' awesome!"

"I know, Chuck! It was awesome!" I reassured him, "It was awesome..."

There was no doubt in my mind that Chuck saw what he saw, but I was also positive if I had elaborated on my visions, he might have thought I was just as nuts as when I used to preach to him about the Bible.

"Sometimes I think I was dreaming it all, Chuck..."

"Oh, you didn't dream it brother! Not unless the two of us had the same fuckin' dream!"

Chuck couldn't contain his excitement or his joy in being able to share his UFO secret with me, but I think he expected me to be a little bit more enthusiastic about having someone to confide in. I, on the other hand, was a bit disappointed that Chuck had so little to report. My band-mate, Mick, had seen several UFO sightings, but had never mentioned seeing anything as spectacular as what I had. I didn't believe either Chuck or Mick had even the slightest clue as to the intensity of what was revealed to me.

For the next two and a half hours, Chuck and I talked about our similar, yet very dissimilar experience, making sure to mention the shape, size, color and speed along with every other detail we could bring to the table about our individual sightings. I was feeling somewhat frustrated because I was yearning to share all my visions with someone, and I thought for sure after Chuck's call he was going to be the one. During the years we worked together, we would get into one unsettled debate after another. He had no tolerance for religion and I thought his claims about extra-terrestrials meddling with life on planet Earth were nothing more than ideas put in his head from watching the Discovery Channel and too many science fiction movies.

There we were exchanging thoughts and ideas about existence, outer space, good and evil, and Chuck was still adamant about his claims that science was the more logical approach to understanding life. Sharing my story about seeing the strange light in the sky not only reinforced Chuck's theories, but allowed him to conclude that we had become sighting comrades. As much as I believed there were other universes and life on other galaxies, I could not convince Chuck that something men respectfully refer to as "God" had something to do with it. I presented him with the idea that maybe religion and what most folks viewed as science fiction were a lot more related than we had ever imagined. Chuck was indeed stubborn and as his eyes glowed with a sinister excitement he said, "Something big is going to happen soon, my friend, I can just feel it…" Pointing heavenward, Chuck continued, "Somebody up there is going to make contact big time!" If Chuck only knew how close he was to the truth.

Chuck grabbed the check, I left the tip. He threw his arms around me and in a tone of genuine affection said, "Don't be a stranger Johnny boy! Stay in touch and keep an eye on the skies!"

~IT'S A SIGN OF THE TIMES~

For over two thousand years, Christians have been waiting for the return of Jesus, as their cry of "Repent, the end is coming soon!" has been passed along from generation to generation. I never believed the delusional Pentecostals' fantasy, in which Jesus would be coming back to Earth riding on a white horse, swinging a sword from one hand, leading all of his faithful followers to glory. I did know, however, that ever since my rendezvous with Chuck, I couldn't stop the premonition it wasn't going to be long until an event so huge was going to bring mankind to its knees. My gut feeling was that planet Earth's immediate future was not looking too bright. Although those suspicions were with me constantly, for some reason I was strangely confident my fate was destined to be quite different. I was experiencing a rather peculiar calmness for someone who may have had a peek at civilization's impending doom. I also knew from way down at the core of my very being that there was nothing I could do to change or stop anything that was going to happen.

Spring was in the air. After experiencing an unusually bad winter, the temperatures were finally climbing into the mid to upper fifties. The gloomy dispositions on the faces of the villagers were turning to smiles as the anticipation of summer seemed to brighten everyone's spirits. I was standing on the Saturday morning bank line at my neighborhood HSBC. Why I chose to deposit a few checks on a busy Saturday morning when I could have easily and more conveniently accomplished that task on any non-busy weekday was anybody's guess. I probably just needed to get out of the house. Jillian and I didn't seem to talk much about anything I found intellectually stimulating. Her world seemed to revolve around housework and church, whereas my world suddenly took on a whole new dimension. I craved a little attention along with some interesting conversation.

An old fashioned guy, not yet an official direct-depositor, I preferred the one-on-one relationship with the bank tellers, engaging them in some uplifting dialogue and sharing a smile or two. Perhaps we were one of the only families in my neighborhood who didn't have any television programming, other than very basic cable, coming into our home. I didn't have the painful pleasure of having the availability of CNN in my face 24-7. One of the perks of standing in line at my bank, aside from the free coffee and donuts, was the strategically positioned HD TV with the ever-present CNN up to the minute news. Customers would become so engrossed in the depressing reports, it took their minds off the long wait; ingenious planning by bank management! Unfortunately, by the time someone finally made his or her way up to the teller's window, he or she was depressed enough to be suicidal. On this particular Saturday morning, the news was nothing shy of devastating.

From the time I left my house, up until the time I reached the nearby bank, tragedy struck the planet once again when a 9.5 earthquake wreaked havoc on Sri Lanka. All transactions came to a halt as customers, tellers and all bank personnel stood paralyzed, mesmerized by the incredible video of the destruction. There was no telling how many deaths had occurred, as once again, the world stood by helplessly witnessing from afar through the magic of television another in a string of recent global catastrophes. Every time a tragic incident like that one arose, and they were occurring more and more regularly, I wondered why such poor nations were the ones being stricken. It wasn't that long ago that Haiti and Indonesia experienced some of the worst disasters the world had ever seen. As much as I was well aware that cataclysmic events such as those were going to be commonplace, I couldn't help but be overly saddened when I saw the suffering and vulnerability on the faces of the victims. It made me furious when I heard religious figureheads claim that such horrifying occurrences were acts of a vengeful God. Although I was relatively sure I had a sneak preview into the future, my heart was painfully stuck in the present.

As I was driving through town on my way home, it became even more apparent the state of our economy was not improving. Storefront after storefront had "For Rent" signs displayed in the windows. Many of the establishments I used to frequent went out of business. It was sad to see Main Street slowly become a ghost town. Foreclosures had become widespread and "For Sale" signs were planted into the front lawns of almost every other house, as many homeowners were left with no alternative than to cash-in and downsize. The entire nation felt the crunch. The rise in unemployment was staggering, the U.S. was still fighting an endless war in the Middle East, and there was yet another far-off country facing natural and economic disaster that we couldn't turn our backs on. Where was the money coming from? Was money even real at that point?

Upon entering my house, I found my wife deeply engaged in a conversation with one of her church friends. From what I could tell, they were talking about the earthquake.

"I don't know Marie, with all that's going on around the world today, I would have to say it certainly seems like the end times," Jillian said somberly. I was only able to imagine the dialogue going on between them and it irritated me to no end…the end of the world, God's wrath, the second coming. The concept of God created by religious denominations drove me absolutely out of my mind. Involuntarily, my humanness kicked in. I tossed the receipts from the bank onto the kitchen table, shook my head in disapproval, took an apple from the fridge and went to sit out on the deck to soak in the sunshine. There was always an underlying tension in the house whenever anything to do with church, religion or spirituality came up. I knew there was no right and no wrong and in the long run, whether we agreed or disagreed, it really didn't matter. It was the arrogant sanctimonious attitude that triggered my exasperation. Squabbling was a waste of time but somehow, I couldn't help myself.

"What's your problem?" Jill demanded, as she made her way outside.

"No problem," I answered while biting down into my crisp Pink Lady, "I don't have a problem; you do!"

"Don't you start with me!" she retaliated, "I could see by the look on your face, you're irritated!"

"Jill, I'm not going to waste my breath," I said calmly, "but when are you going to wake up? It pains me to know that you and all your 'Brothers and Sisters in the Lord' are so sadly misguided and in the clutches of an insane belief system. How do you think it makes me feel knowing you refuse to even consider the possibility you might be wrong! How is it the least bit feasible everybody else on the planet is mistaken and only you and your fellow followers are right…It's illogical! It's madness!"

"Oh yeah!" she blurted out sarcastically, "and you expect me to take you seriously when you talk about flying saucers and E.T.'s?"

"Makes more sense than your fairytales about Hell and the devil," I shot back at her rather emphatically, "Christians have been waiting for Jesus for over two thousand years…He ain't been back yet and He ain't coming back the way you think He is!"

"Say whatever you want, I believe God! I go by what it says in the Bible!" she replied with unconvincing confidence.

"I don't want to argue," I said in what I knew was a futile comeback, "But one of these days you'll get it, and I'm telling you, you are going to be in for the surprise of your life!"

I was extremely disappointed over my moment of weakness. Arguing was pointless, but that's pretty much how things went in our lives. We lived together, slept together, raised two kids, paid the bills, and played house. Although deep down I knew we cared for each other, as far as discussing anything concerning religion and spiritual growth, we had become so totally incompatible that it seemed almost hopeless. Knowing what I knew made it even harder for me. At one time I had swallowed the same misconceptions she refused to even question. I loved Jillian and desperately craved to share my visions with her, assuming that's all it would take to bridge the gap and restore our marriage to the way it was decades ago. What would be the purpose in my wanting to deceive her? Whatever journey I was about to embark on, I wanted Jill at my side, but I had the sinking feeling in my heart it wasn't in the cards. Maybe it was fear that led to her inflexible mindset and kept her from entertaining any ideas deviating from her comfort zone. Although I saw how superstition and guilt have snared millions into defending faith, I also recognized Jillian had her own path to follow and in her eyes I was the rebellious, stubborn one.

~A BEAUTIFUL DAY IN THE NEIGHBORHOOD~

Upon waking up every morning, I couldn't help but wonder what the day was going to bring. I felt an acute alertness about myself I had never been able to experience before. Sights and sounds were sharper, clearer and more defined. I was able to sense the positive and negative vibrations coming from the people around me. I became extremely sensitive to the feelings of others, perceiving their compassion, fear, anxiety, stubbornness and hopefulness. It was quite strange and a bit wearisome having to keep many of my deep-seated thoughts to myself. It was also very unsettling to know how many people, including friends, family and acquaintances, were so asleep. The majority of the population had no time to think about anything other than making a living, getting laid and getting over. Religious extremists of all faiths were doing their utmost to instill fear and hate around a confused planet and were succeeding at it. The insane minorities had always managed to wreak havoc amongst the unsuspectingly distracted majorities.

The news continued to fill us in on all the latest stories regarding the usual despicable acts of human behavior. Murder, robbery, rape, extortion, and general cruelty still sold papers and attracted viewers. The first thing Jill did on a daily basis was to get out of bed and immediately turn on the television. The handsome anchormen and shapely anchor-women, along with their teams of on-location news reporters, turned my stomach so much that I've had to leave the room. They were like media prostitutes, high paid pretty boys and girls who screwed with peoples' minds, filling their heads with negativity, disasters and horror. So often I had suspected it was all a well-calculated scheme to keep the masses terrified. I would always lay into Jillian and condemn her for wasting her time glued to the TV.

"How do you watch that shit?" I'd question as if demanding an answer, "You're starting your day off with such depression!"

"Don't tell me what to watch…I want to see what the weather's going to be like!" she'd retort.

"Why don't you just step outside and find out for yourself?" I'd snap back, "…and turn off that fuckin' television for a change!"

I found it extremely frustrating how Jill seemed to pay more attention to the broadcasting networks than to what I had to say. I imagined it was her way to escape my opposition and continuous criticism of her beliefs.

It was no different than any other day. The stench of resentment filling the air should have gagged us. She went about watching her morning array of mind-numbing TV programs while I did my very best to block out the irritating sound of studio audience forced laughter and fake applause. I almost hated myself for the way I succumbed to our spiteful behavior. I knew in both my heart and mind, Love was the only way to settle any-thing, yet I couldn't take my own advice. I felt like quite the hypocrite, talking the talk without walking the walk, as they say. Sometimes I would wonder whether or not I had become just as strong-headed as she was. If that were true, it was only because I had proof. I absolutely saw what I saw. I had difficulty in understanding how people like Jillian had no problem accepting second-hand stories about the dreams of long dead

Bible characters of yesteryear, yet held absolutely no credibility for the dreams of the living.

I decided to get out of the house for a while. The weather was great... blue sky, plenty of sunshine. A walk was definitely going to do me good. I needed to get out into the fresh air to try and get my thoughts in order. I wasn't happy about the ridiculous uneasiness and tension in our relationship but I knew I had to be true to myself. I was a seeker, always questioning things. It was my nature. I felt that as long as I was around Jill, in order for us to live amiably I had to refrain from faith-threatening probing discussions because, somehow, they always led to arguments and insults. The very thing that drove me, my reason for living, seemed to be stifled in my own home. As much as I knew that Jill stood firmly by her convictions, what evidence did she have? Childhood indoctrination and years of Sunday morning brainwashing sessions could not measure up to the magnificence of what I saw. I knew the stress in our marriage wasn't at all healthy for either of us, but I also knew, even with the indifference we felt towards each other, as unwarranted as it may have been, leaving her would be painful. We shared a long history that included raising two wonderful kids.

The trees were just beginning to bloom. Crocuses were awakening from their winter-long slumber and the matted down front lawns throughout my neighborhood were slowly springing back to life. The rebirth of the flowers, plants, shrubs and trees amazed me. Every autumn I would get a little saddened to see the leaves on the trees surrender their vibrant green color then fall to the ground in lifeless piles waiting to be gathered and carried away to burn. The colorful petals of the flowers once bordering the landscapes along the suburban streets lost their brilliance, and as if they were gasping for a last breath of air, relinquished their will to cling to the fragile stems, and dropped to fuse with the soil. With the reckless whacks of the landscapers' blades and the swift strokes of their rakes, all signs of summer were gone. Spring, however, meant resurrection and all we assumed was dead returned to life.

As I walked, I got an unexplainable feeling of positivity and hope, observing all the indications that June, July and August were not too far away. There was a quiet little park on the south side of my town, so I decided that would be my destination. For more than half my life I lived in a small Long Island village known as Lakeside. I thought Lakeside was an odd name because there were absolutely no lakes anywhere in the vicinity. There was a huge bay that led to the ocean and numerous canals, but positively no lakes. Lakeside was an unassuming diverse community largely inhabited by blue collar workers and fishermen. I was born and raised in New York City, so living in Lakeside was rather a dramatic change for me. I guess the primary reason we chose to live there was its affordability and the fact that the people were down-to-earth. It was by no means "keeping–up–with–the–Jones'" territory. Jillian, the kids, and I loved living in Lakeside.

I was standing on the northwest corner of Waterside Avenue and Constellation Road waiting for the traffic light to change. It was unusually busy for a weekday. Ordinarily I'd just have to look both ways, not pay much attention to the signals, and leisurely make my way across the road. On that particular day, I was in no hurry, so I patiently stood there until the flashing red "Don't Walk" warning sign changed to green, indicating it was safe to "Walk." Standing beside me, balancing a beat up bicycle, the kind with a banana seat and motorcycle-style handlebars, looking like it was purchased at a garage sale, was a boy I recognized from the area. He appeared to be at most sixteen years old, had shoulder length straight blond hair, deep blue eyes and was obviously in a hurry. Clad in loose-fitting shorts drooping below his knees and a black faded oversized

"Rolling Stones" tee-shirt that had to be a hand-me-down from someone more my age, he was surely jumping the gun on summer. He fidgeted, continually looking both ways, never once paying the slightest attention to the "Don't Walk" sign. Twice he made attempts to cut across the road, but mindfully calculating the speed of the oncoming automobiles, wisely hesitated.

When our eyes met, he nodded politely and said, "Hey, how you doing?"

I figured he must have recognized me. I nodded back and said in somewhat of an authoritative tone of voice, "You better be careful, man, don't want to lose your life because you didn't wait a few more seconds!" He smiled, displaying perfect teeth, then after quickly positioning himself on the bike, he swiftly zipped out into the intersection, like a getaway car fleeing from a crime scene.

In life, timing was everything. It all happened so suddenly. He looked both ways. The coast was clear. Seconds before the bicycle made it across to the opposite corner, the deafening screech and the repellent stench of a car burning rubber filled the air, followed by a sudden sickly thud. A poorly painted aquamarine Honda Civic peeled out from a Dunkin' Donuts parking lot, obviously trying to beat the light, and struck the boy on the bike, sending him sailing through the air for several feet. Merchants and shoppers from the stores in the immediate area came rushing out to the street. "Oh my God!" women gasped, while their children stood by, crying in fear at the sight of young body lying bleeding in the roadway. Folks were calling for help on their cell phones, cars were pulling over as civilians attempted to direct traffic.

I don't know what came over me, but I pushed my way through the small crowd and ran directly to the boy as if I were some sort of miracle man. Strangely, all the Bible indoctrination I endured years ago immediately came to mind. I thought about all the unproven tales, where in situations such as the one I was in defenders of the faith cried out in the name of Jesus for a miraculous healing. I'd never seen it work for me or for anyone else, yet I felt compelled to lay my hands upon the child in the same way the Asian girl did to her stricken father at the bar. No one attempted to stop me as I knelt beside him. Blood was trickling down from above his hairline, creating what looked like red tributaries upon his face. He was motionless, except for the slight pulsing of his chest, indicating he was breathing faintly. It seemed as though he was clutching, trying desperately to hang on and keep from being sucked into another realm. I don't think I could ever accurately explain what I experienced at that moment. I sensed compassion in a way I'd never known. Every vibrating cell of my being yearned for nothing more than to take away the fear and the pain from that young boy. I felt at any second my eyes were going to gush with tears. My body became incredibly warm...the heat seemed to radiate from deep within my gut outwards...my hands were on fire. I knew something supernatural was working through me...something nameless, wonderful, and powerful. I gently placed my hands upon the boy's temple and lowered my body as to get as close to him as possible. At that point, I momentarily lost any awareness of who I was, like on the day of the sighting. Every ounce of my energy bonded with his... for a split second, we were one.

As his eyes opened wide, he reached for my hand. Not too far off in the distance I heard the screaming of ambulance and police car sirens. Did it take them that long to arrive, or did everything that happened just happen so quickly? Wherever it was I briefly transcended, it seemed as though I was back almost instantly. "Are you alright?" I softly spoke. The boy nodded and smiled, once again displaying his flawless white teeth.

"I should've listened to you, man! Where's my bike?"

"Never mind your bike," I answered, "You're lucky to be alive!"

"I guess it's just not my time," he replied grinning, "God still needs me here for something!"

While he slowly and carefully lifted himself into a sitting position, the EMT's came rushing to the scene with a stretcher. "Is he okay?" a slightly overweight technician asked in a rather routine fashion.

"I think he's going to be fine," I answered confidently and asked for a wet cloth in order to wipe the blood from the boy's face.

Two police cars arrived at the scene and the four officers who emerged from those cars split themselves up among the onlookers. One of them went directly to interrogate the driver and passenger of the Civic, while the others solicited witnesses and directed traffic. From the corner of my eye, I saw a very animated woman, who I had to guess was in her sixties, pointing directly at me as her lips were moving wildly. I could only imagine what her interpretation of the event might have been. Just then, the officer and the young man who struck the bicyclist approached us. I could tell the driver of the vehicle was quite shaken, his dark complexion turning almost ghostly.

"Are you alright?" the fellow asked nervously with a very noticeable Hispanic accent, "I'm so sorry, I didn't see you…Thank God, I thought I killed you, man!"

"For a second or so, I thought you did too," the boy answered and repeated, "I thought you did too!"

The cop, who looked like a kid himself, his stiff navy blue uniform appearing a size or so too large for him, directed his question to me.

"Are you guys related?"

Before I even had the chance to part my lips to answer, my new friend cut in, "Yeah, he's my uncle!"

The out of shape EMT guy quickly scanned the kid's body, and then after examining him a little closer asked the same question I was thinking, "Where did all that blood come from?" He looked totally confused and recommended we get into the back of the ambulance so he could take the boy to the hospital to get checked out. Upon hearing the suggestion, the apparently uninjured kid jumped to his feet and said, "I'm fine, just a few scratches…no need for any doctors!"

"Gracias a Dios," the driver blurted out joyously, thinking only moments ago his immediate future was a jail cell.

The kid tugged on my arm and spoke softly in my ear, "Just tell them all to go, I'm fine. As for you, we need to talk!"

Crazy as it sounds, before the police arrived, I didn't think the kid had a chance. The way he was thrown from that bike, the impact of the car and the amount of blood oozing from his head, I assumed he was a goner. He stood before me without a bruise on his body…almost perfect. The only signs that he was just in an accident were the grime from the street and the blood stains on his clothes. The accounts from the eyewitnesses had the police looking as dumbfounded as the medical technician.

"So what are we doing here," one of the befuddled police officers inquired impatiently, "are we going to the hospital or not?"

"I think he's fine officer, thank God! No need to complicate matters! I'll take him home."

While the one cop seemed to struggle with how to fill in the details of the accident report, another carried the mangled bicycle to the sidewalk shaking his head in bewilderment as he probably wondered how the kid survived. With the boy holding on to my arm as if I really were his uncle, the two of us walked towards the very same corner we met, as the remaining bystanders gave us baffled looks and strange gazes.

"So, what do you think happened back there?" he questioned me as if he already knew the answer.

"What did you feel?" I asked.

"I thought I was going to die," he told me without hesitation, "I saw bright lights, you know, the kind people say they see when they're, you know..."

"What else did you see," I interrupted.

"Just total blackness and blinding light," he answered with certainty, as though he'd experienced this sort of thing before. Then he continued, "It was the heat I remember the most, I felt like I was burning, yet it felt so good...Then there was just dark emptiness, like floating in space, and a warm peacefulness followed by the brightest light...like staring directly into the sun," he said as his eyes widened and his head and hands shook uncontrollably.

He went on, pulling from his memory whatever he could grab hold of. "It's hard to explain exactly, but I kind of sensed a peacefulness as I kept getting hotter and hotter, like my insides were on fire, yet it was, uh, weird, I wasn't frightened or anything...then my eyes opened and I saw you...but it was like I knew you were there all along...Hey man, who are you? How did you do that?"

Realizing we didn't even know each other's name, I extended my hand and formally introduced myself, "Hi, I'm John, and I'm trying to figure it out myself!"

The kid gripped my hand firmly and said, "Hey John, I'm Brian, thanks for, well, whatever it is you did...I guess you kind of saved my life or at least from a stay in the hospital!"

Pointing to the twisted remains of his bicycle and knowing my question was pointless, I asked, "Do you want to take that with you?"

"Nah!" he replied, smiling and waving his arm as if he could care less, then continued, "I found it in the garbage...I'll find another one!"

"So where do you live?" I inquired, "I'll walk you home. I think we kind of need to talk a bit."

"I live on Maple," he said, "Between Parkside and Prince."

"Oh! I'm only two blocks from there," I responded, "...on Elm...I thought I'd seen you around."

As we seemed to purposely take our time returning to our homes, walking back along the same route I took earlier, I once again marveled at all the new growth rising up from the earth. "Pretty amazing," I exclaimed!

"What's amazing?" he asked curiously.

"Nature," I said grinning, while directing his attention to the daffodils breaking through the dark brown soil, "Just nature, the way life continues..."

"You know what's amazing?" he asked and answered immediately, "What just happened back there...that's what's freaking amazing...Tell me man, you did something...you're the reason I'm walking right now... What the fuck happened?"

"Brian," I said, "as soon as I figure it all out, I'll be sure to let you know!"

We walked in circles, going up and down the same streets, doing the best we could to keep the conversation alive because neither of us wanted to go home. Having never gone through anything of that magnitude before, I was just as dazzled as Brian about the day's events. I could tell he didn't know exactly what to make of me, but I also knew he wasn't going to leave my side until he did. He began to tell me a little bit about his personal life, mentioning that his parents were divorced.

"A year or so after my Dad moved out," he explained, "my Mom joined this crazy church. She dragged me with her there a few times, but they all looked like they were nuts to me…jumping and yelling…"

"Yeah," I sympathized, "Been there, done that…"

As if he were the one leading the way, he quickly walked a little bit past me, turned to face me and stopped me from walking any further. "Are you one of those church dudes my Mom's always talking about… you know, the kind who can heal somebody?"

"Kid," I laughed, "I haven't stepped foot inside a church in years!" I motioned for us to continue walking and as an unmistakable assuredness swelled up inside my being I said, "Brian, can you keep a secret?"

~A PICTURE'S WORTH A THOUSAND WORDS~

We leisurely rambled up, down, and around the streets bordering our homes like a plane circling the skies waiting for permission to land. Engrossed in conversation, we unknowingly sauntered half-way down Maple Street until Brian said, "Hey, this is my house!" and we landed ourselves seats on his front stoop. I must have driven past it at least a hundred times. The house was a modest little cape with a thirsty front lawn, overgrown shrubs, rusted railings and shutters that cried out for a fresh coat of paint.

Prior to arriving at his home, when we strolled about the immediate neighborhood, Brian relentlessly pleaded with me to disclose how I was able to do what I did and I reassured him I would try my best to do so after I got to know him a little better. I learned he was sixteen, a senior at Lakeside High and an only child. Brian unhappily explained how his Mom and Dad seemed to live in two completely different worlds. His mother was a nurse at the county hospital who, in a teenager's perspective, always looked weary and unhappy, possibly because of all the long hours she worked, possibly because his Dad never gave her any attention. He bemoaned how he could never recall his Mom and Dad ever spending any quality time together. His Mom was always tired from working double shifts, so the three of them rarely sat down as a family to eat or even watch TV. He told me how his parents never seemed to communicate much and he wondered how they ever got together in the first place. "My Mom goes about her life and my Dad goes about his. I pretty much learned how to take care of myself," he said matter-of-factly, "We all have to do what we have to do!" My heart was aching for this kid, yet I knew he was right. We all have to do what we have to do.

He portrayed his mother as a very rigid, all work and no play woman, not anywhere near as imaginative as his creative father. I thought to myself, "Opposites may attract, but they undoubtedly clash." He seemed to speak highly of his Dad, describing him to be the unconventional type, an under-appreciated artist who lived to draw and paint but could not make a living by doing what he loved to do.

"He never had a steady job, and although he did whatever was necessary to help pay the bills, everything from driving a taxi to painting houses to landscaping, I really think he resented it. I guess he always hoped that someday he was going to be known for his paintings and make his fortune," Brian said admiringly. "Hey, you want to see some of his stuff?"

"Sure," I answered cautiously, "Are you sure it's okay for me to come in?"

"Yeah," he answered confidently, "My Mom's at work and even if she were home, she wouldn't care. I show off my Dad's artwork all the time!"

Brian led me through his unlocked front door. We passed through a living room cluttered with books, magazines and Bible study guides and into a kitchen with a sink full of dirty pots and dishes. "Don't mind the mess," he directed, "I didn't get to the dishes yet…that's my job and Mom's working late tonight, so I've got time!" Just behind the kitchen was a small enclosed porch and proudly displayed upon every square inch of wall space were his Dad's paintings. They were absolutely extraordinary.

I moved slowly about the room as if I were in an art gallery, astonished by his brilliant work.

"My God," I cried out, "These are incredible!"

Brian, happy to see I approved, called out, "Check this one out…" and revealed a 3 foot by 5 foot painting that had been hiding behind an old worn-out couch. My eyes opened as wide as they possibly could when I beheld the most magnificent life-like canvas of a flying saucer hovering overhead the village of Lakeside. I stood there mesmerized and instantly flashed back to my encounter as a rush of illuminating images flooded my head.

"Are you alright?" Brian questioned, the sound of his voice grounding me.

"Yeah, Brian, I'm fine…this is absolutely remarkable…where is your Dad? I'd love to talk with him."

Brian began to tell the story I'm sure he's told time and time again. "A few years ago my Dad met a woman from Brazil who admired his work and one by one, she began to buy several of his paintings. At first, she would come by just once in a while and then her visits became more frequent. I think my Mom suspected they may have been falling in love. The Brazilian lady would hang around and tell my Mom how wonderful my Dad was and how lucky she was to be married to such a deeply talented man, the kind of encouragement my Dad never heard from my Mom. I guess after a while he did fall in love with her, because the two of them left for South America and never came back. He calls now and then and we talk. He apologizes to me every time we do, asks for my forgiveness and lets me know that he's very happy. 'Be happy for me, Brian,' he says, and how am I supposed to respond to that?"

"That must have hurt," I said compassionately, "It had to be rough for you and your Mom…"

"Yeah," he continued, telling the story as if it were therapeutic for him, "My Mom took it kind of bad, which I couldn't understand because their marriage kind of sucked anyway."

After carefully placing the painting back behind the couch, Brian resumed his story. "Not too long after Dad split, Mom joined a divorcee support group at that church down where Constellation and Jefferson intersect…You know where I mean, right?"

"Sure," I answered, "I know it well! Sat in on a few services there years ago…"

"Well, once she started attending that church, all she'd ever do is read her Bible and pester me to do the same. She dragged me with her to some of those crazy services where people do to sick folks what you did to me…that's why I thought…"

"No, Brian," I reassured him, I think I'm more on the same page with your Dad!"

"I miss him, you know? It kind of sucks not having him around even though he was always kind of off in his own world all the time."

"It sure seems like your Dad was quite an interesting guy," I said supportively, "He certainly is very talented!" With a good deal of my attention still on that painting, I couldn't help but wonder if what Brian's Dad had so explicitly brought to life on canvas was something he actually saw or something from out of his imagination.

"Okay, so I told you something about me," Brian quipped, "Now you've got to tell me who you are and how you did what you did!"

"Alright, my friend," I said agreeing, "But this stays strictly between us!"

"Shoot!" he promised as he listened attentively.

Brian and I took the return trip through the house and back to his front stoop where I unfolded my story beginning with the occurrence on the night of December 10th and culminating with our not-so-chance meeting and the supernatural incident that happened just hours ago on Waterside.

"Holy shit," Brian snapped, "Then my Dad really did see what he painted!"

"It's very likely," I said, "It's very likely! Now you just keep that story between the two of us or else they may put us both away!"

I gave Brian a firm handshake and a quick friendly hug and said, "If I don't get home they're going to send a search party after me."

While looking down and aimlessly kicking some broken twigs onto the lawn, he said with an appreciative grin, "It was good talking to you, Uncle John! You know where I live now…Stop by once in a while!"

"Same here, my friend, the pleasure was all mine! Hope to see you soon!"

As I headed home, my insides were jumping with excitement at the sight of that painting, yet my heart was breaking because I had no one with whom to share my excitement.

~MAKES FOR GOOD DINNER CONVERSATION~

When I finally made it back home, dinner was almost ready. Upon entering the house, I could smell the heavenly scent of garlic being sautéed in olive oil and at the same time, I sensed the negativity emanating from Jill. She was obviously annoyed that I had disappeared for a good part of the afternoon and she was going to be certain that I knew it. If it weren't for the fact she loved to eat, she probably wouldn't have cooked. But since she enjoyed experimenting in the kitchen by preparing different dishes, and thanks to her new affection for the Rachel Ray show, I enjoyed the benefits.

"Where the heck were you?" she asked, grilling me like an interrogating officer, "What did you do, get lost?"

"Can't a guy take a walk?" I answered apologetically with a slight touch of sarcasm, "Besides, you're the one who keeps telling me I need to exercise…"

"Didn't you realize the time? Didn't you think dinner would be ready?" she drilled relentlessly, "I could've used your help!"

There was no sense in arguing, so I answered calmly, "I'm home…I'll set the table and call the kids so we could eat." I placed the dishes on the table then hollered up the stairs leading to their bedrooms, "Sam! Daniel! Dinner's ready!"

"Isn't it ridiculous that you have to set the table?" Jill lectured, "Your kids think this is a hotel and we're the caretakers!"

"I'll talk to them," I said, mistakenly thinking I might appease her.

"A lot of good that's ever done!" she shot back.

It was so illogical how Jill would unleash her wrath on me simply for assuming what I was thinking, yet never take interest enough to ask me what was really going on in my head. Sometimes I just had to let her vent. Sooner or later whatever was pissing her off would blow over. As we finally took our seats around the dinner table, while pouring some wine into Jill's glass, I said, "I saw a nasty accident down on Constellation this afternoon."

"What happened?" Sam asked, suddenly interested.

I described to my family, omitting a few of the very important details, the potentially ugly scene I had witnessed earlier in the day. I hated not being able to share the day's inexplicable events, but I figured it would have been better for all of us if they never found out. God knows how Jill would have tried to rationalize the healing ability of a heathen, especially when I even had no clue. Anything that did not conform to her dogma was conveniently Satanic.

"I know that kid!" Daniel exclaimed, "He lives a few blocks from here...I think his parents are separated."

"Divorced," I added, "They're divorced!"

"How do you know?" Jill wondered out loud.

"Uh, Bald Joe from the deli told me...he knows the kid's mother," I answered, "Want to know anything about anybody around here, just ask Bald Joe!"

"Is he alright?" Jill asked.

"Who, Joe," I asked jokingly.

"No, you idiot," Jill shrieked not thinking I was funny, "The boy!"

"Yeah…he's fine! Kids are so resilient…it was amazing how he just got up and walked away…So, how was your day, guys," I quickly questioned, trying to change the subject, "Anything new?" I could only have imagined the reaction I would've gotten if I told them what really happened…

The truth of it was, at the time, I wasn't sure if I even knew what had happened. All I could assume was that there was definitely a connection between what occurred in that parking lot on December 10th and what transpired on Constellation Road that very afternoon. An entity, very mysterious and very powerful, had certainly succeeded in getting my attention. As to why, I was exceedingly anxious to find out.

~FAMILY SECRETS~

Sometimes I used to think if it weren't for occasions such as birthdays and the like, I would've never seen my parents or my siblings. July was upon us once again and my Dad was celebrating, or trying not to celebrate, his 87th birthday. It had become a custom through the years, when my brother and two sisters, along with their spouses and children, all congregated at the house we grew up in to honor our parents' birthdays. As much as my Dad moaned and groaned about all of us having to disrupt our busy schedules and travel considerable distances just to watch him blow out a candle and make a wish, I think he loved it. By the time the birthday cake was served, however, I would almost bet the only wish he made was that we'd all go home.

Veterans of the Old World school of thought, yet enlightened enough to be tolerant of the New, both my folks not only looked great for their age, they were uncommonly open-minded with an appreciation for thought-provoking conversation. Their youthfulness could partly be attributed to keeping up with the latest trends and never giving into that old-age mindset. Year after year, my Dad would remind us, "Age is just a state of mind!" I found it commendable, how after being together for all those years, my Mom and Dad were still genuinely in love. The glow in their eyes revealed it.   Even into their upper eighties they were never ashamed to show each other outward signs of affection. They truly enjoyed one another's company and their playful antics led me to believe they were still having sex regularly.

Things had changed quite a bit during the years. My sister Theresa got divorced after twenty-six years of marriage and raising three kids. It was hard getting used to not having my ex-brother-in-law Phil in the picture any longer. I had more in common with him than I did with my own sister. Since there are three sides to every divorce story, I couldn't harbor any ill feelings towards Phil. I think I was sadder for me than I was for Theresa. Besides, in all probability, she drove him out the door. Even when we were kids she was a pain in the ass. We never did get the whole story, but would it have mattered if we did? Phil had always been a good Dad and continued to see to it that my nieces and nephew were taken care of. Theresa got to keep the house and as far as I knew, she hadn't dated since Phil left, seeming quite content to be on her own. Phil took an apartment in the city and the last time I ran into him he was accompanied by a much younger woman. I must admit he seemed pretty happy.

Of course, all the grandchildren have gotten older and the last thing they wanted to do was to disrupt their social calendar by wasting the precious hours of a weekend with their elderly grandfather. I considered myself pretty lucky to have had both my parents significantly healthy and still kicking into their late eighties. As much as I'd grown to dislike the prisons we'd created for ourselves with traditions, sometimes I was glad I didn't abandon all of them. Even with the confusion and occasional disharmony among so many family members, it was good, in a way, to sit around the same dinner table I sat at as a child, and get to converse and reminisce with my crazy siblings.

Mark was the younger brother. Growing up, his sisters used to spoil the crap out of him and for reasons I never understood, his wife Abby did too. I don't believe I was ever jealous of him, I just didn't understand it. He wasn't the most likable guy, and though it pains me to admit that about my own brother, it was true. He was opinionated, sarcastic and condescending; humility was definitely not one of his virtues. Mark and Abby opted not to have children. He had never been able to hold down a job for any length of time so he decided to go for his real estate license with the hopes of opening his own agency. She, on the other hand, was a VP for Citibank. Choosing a career over motherhood, she essentially supported the two of them with her hefty six-figure salary while he fumbled at selling houses. What was even more puzzling to me was how absolutely stunning Abby was. She could have had any man she desired. How and why she ever settled for Mark had always been a mystery to me. Who can account for taste?

My sister Diane and her husband David had been married a little over thirty-two years. They had four kids, two of each. Diane and Theresa were night and day. Diane was the sweetest, most compassionate person alive. She was at one time a Special Ed teacher who loved her job, but hadn't worked a day since she became a Mom. With Diane, I was never quite sure if her giving religiously to at least a dozen different charities and her almost perfect attendance record at church on Sunday was a result of guilt, superstition or genuine faith. As long as he was free to golf, go to baseball, football and hockey games, and pretty much do as he pleased, David didn't seem to care what she did or how she spent money.

David was one of those Wall Street cats who made a fortune. On the surface he seemed to treat my sister pretty well. They lived in a well-to-do community on the North Shore of Long Island. My sister always drove the finest cars. My nieces and nephews went to the best schools. Somehow though, there was something about David that made me uncomfortable. I always had the gut feeling he'd been cheating on Diane. I knew better than to judge or to assume, and I completely understood as to why infidelity occurs, but I just didn't want to see my sister get hurt. The way I perceived it, she was too good a person, almost angelic. Whatever works, I guess. Maybe money does buy happiness.

It was out of the ordinary for Jillian not to be by my side at these annual events, but on this particular night, she was truly not feeling well and decided to not spread her germs around by staying home. If I explained where she was once, I explained it a thousand times. Sometimes I thought my siblings were just dying to hear me say I was having marital problems.

Dad just completed the make-a-wish candle-blowing ceremony when Diane said, "Remember the way Uncle Pete always used to get grossed out when anybody blew out candles on a cake?"

"Yeah, rest his soul," Theresa chimed in, "He was quite the character! Mom always had to put plastic wrap on top of the cake whenever there was any candle-blowing going on or else he wouldn't eat the cake!"

"Actually, that was wise on his part," I added, "You never know what sort of germs could have attached themselves to the frosting!"

Uncle Pete was married to my Dad's sister Ruth. A tall, boney, relatively handsome man with deep set hazel eyes and from what I recall, a terrific sense of humor, towered above my pint-sized serious-natured aunt. He grew his hair unusually long for someone of his generation and I think he did so just to demonstrate his mid-life rebelliousness to practically everything. Aunt Ruth had died about ten years before Pete did, but since he regarded my Dad more of a brother than an in-law, they continued to remain very close. The one thing I vividly remember was how my aunt and uncle never saw eye to eye on anything concerning religion. No matter how my aunt begged, my uncle refused to step foot into a house of worship. He had been so opposed to religion and anything relating to it, he didn't even attend the church ceremony for any of our weddings. He had no tolerance when it came to organized religion and he always used to say, "There's over fifty thousand religious sects in the world and not one of them is even close to the truth!" Maybe he's the one I got it from.

My Mom lived for these gatherings. She used to love it when all her kids were together pretending to be close by taking fake interest in one another's lives. "I loved your Uncle Pete, kids, but I have to say, one day he just wasn't his old self anymore. He became most peculiar," my Mom spoke warily, wearing one of her "I know something you don't know" grins.

"I know he may have had a few eccentricities, but what was so peculiar about him, Mom? I don't remember him that way!" I asked curiously.

"When you kids moved out and were on your own, your uncle stopped coming around as often as he used to. Your father and I wondered if the only reason he came around was to see you guys." After quickly glancing over at my Dad, my Mom continued, "Whenever he did visit, as soon as it got dark, he would wander off into the backyard alone, smoke a cigarette or two and just watch the sky. He never said much, just stared into the heavens as if he were waiting for something. After about thirty minutes or so, he'd come back into the house and say, 'Nothing tonight!' then say no more."

"Maybe he just liked to get some fresh air, it's always so freakin' hot in here," Theresa said in her usual unkind brand of sarcasm.

"If you're hot Theresa, take off your sweater, it's comfortable in here! Do you think it's hot in here, John?" Mom asked.

"No, Ma, it's fine…so what about poor Uncle Pete?"

"Well one night I asked him why he was always looking up in the sky and he gave me this look and said, 'You wouldn't understand Marian, you'd just think I was crazy,' but I kept hounding him until he spit it out…"

Before Mom could reveal the mysterious news about my favorite uncle, my Dad blurted in, "Damn it Marian, let the man rest in peace… don't shatter their image of the man for Christ's sake…"

"Michael," Mom said calmly, "It's not that bad…you're acting like I was making him out to be…"

"Crazy!" my Dad yelled, "You're going to make them think he was crazy!"

"Dad," Diane, Theresa and I cried out in unison, "Let Mom tell her story!"

"Thank you, kids," Mom nodded and went on with her tale. "Your Uncle Pete confided in me and your Dad, in fact, he didn't even tell your Aunt Ruth, that one night on the way home from working a late shift, he claimed to have seen one of those flying saucers…"

My insides did a quick flip and a hot flash streaked through my body as soon as I heard my Mom utter the words, "flying saucer." I felt the heat rise up to my head as my face must have turned considerably red.

"Are you alright, John, you looked flushed," my Mom asked caringly, "You want some water…"

"See, Mom, it is hot in here," Theresa cut in.

"No, Mom, it's okay, I'm good," I reassured her, "go on!"

Mom waited to make sure we were all listening attentively before continuing. "Well after he told us he saw a flying saucer, he looked closely at our faces to make sure we weren't going to laugh. I mean, I figured it was very possible he saw something, you know, a shooting star, an airplane… but then he told us that he actually thought he made contact with some sort of alien being…he said it spoke to him…"

"Come on," David said almost impatiently, "You don't believe that, do you Mom?"

"I have to say," Mom went on rather earnestly, "Even your Dad will agree, ever since the day he divulged to us about, you know, really communicating with an…"

"What?" Theresa interrupted, "He talked to them?"

"Kids," Mom resumed, "Your Uncle swore up and down that some other life force communicated with him. Supposedly, it told him they've been here before, and that they come back frequently to guide us…If it weren't for the drastic change in him, I wouldn't have believed it…but suddenly he seemed to be a wealth of information…he just knew things he never let on he knew before…Well, now I'm afraid you're all going to think I'm the crazy one…"

"Don't be ridiculous, Mom," I said excitedly, "I want to hear more… what else did he tell you?"

"Well John," Mom softly spoke, "He tried to explain how, uh, does anybody want more coffee?"

"Ma," Mark yelled, "Finish your story, please! I've got to get home sometime tonight!"

"Mark, honey," Abby chirped, "Be nice and let your Mom continue speaking…"

"Uncle Pete tried to explain how there are alien civilizations much more intelligent and sophisticated than, you know, us earthlings…He said they evolved to a consciousness level that enabled them to do things that we would consider miraculous…He said that they allowed him to see the past and the future as if they had God-like qualities…"

"Alright Mom, now you're sounding a little bit nuts," Diane said lovingly, "Maybe Uncle Pete lost it in his old age…"

"Your uncle was perfectly sane...He held to his story until the day he died..."

Just then, Dad got up from the table and after taking a few moments to straighten up, slowly walked over to stand behind Mom. "I never dreamed I'd be standing here talking to my children about flying saucers, aliens and God on the same breath, but your mother's not making this stuff up...Pete was never the same...He definitely saw something. I can't say for sure what the hell he saw, but that's all he ever had on his mind... it was like he was in a trance all the time...always re-enacting that night in his head..."

While my brother and sisters were looking at our parents like they were about to cry out "April Fools," I was thinking about how I could prod them for more information.

"You know," I said, "Lately I've been reading a lot of books affirming the same kind of stuff Uncle Pete was trying to convey..."

"What, now you're on a Martian kick?" Mark commented while stuffing a chocolate chip cookie into his mouth, "One day you're into Jesus, the next day you're into Gandhi, now you're into Martians! What's next my impressionable brother?"

The last thing I wanted to do was start a debate and I knew if I told them about what I had seen, Mark would start in. I also knew I had to obey my instincts and not talk about it. Something, however, was encouraging me to let my Mom in on my little secret.

"Mark," I answered calmly, "Who knows what's out there? Surely you can't believe that human beings are the only intelligent life in the universe...and I use the word intelligent loosely!"

"Fuck you, John boy!" Mark snapped back at me.

"Mark!" Mom reprimanded, "Don't talk to your brother like that!"

"It's okay, Mom, I'm used to it," I said, unaffected by his remark, "But back to what I was saying…There's so much interesting information out there about extra-terrestrials and the likelihood that higher life forms do exist. Some theorists believe the reason they are so advanced is because they were able to, sort of connect with, uh, let's call it God! I mean, didn't Jesus say that we too should be performing miracles even greater than his?"

"I got to go Ma! I had enough," Mark shouted while reaching for Abby's hand, "Come on babe, my brother's fucking nuts!"

"Mark!" Mom cried out, "Enough with that language!"

On that note, everybody started getting restless and moved away from the table. Diane pointed to the clock while staring at her husband, making sure he caught her unmistakable signal it was time to hit the road. Dad thanked everybody for coming while one by one they all hesitantly marched out the front door, kissing and hugging in what always ended up as the everlasting exiting ceremony. I stayed behind to help the folks with the dishes. They always tried to push me out the door, assuring me that they could handle the clean up, but I knew my Mom appreciated my hanging around.

As I placed the last few coffee cups into the dishwasher, I looked at my Mom and said, "Why didn't you ever mention this stuff about Uncle Pete before?"

"Because it just never came up and your father thought it best not to…"

"You know, Mom…I know what Uncle Pete was going through…I, uh…"

"Go on, John; say what you were going to say," Mom said encouragingly, "I believed your uncle really saw something…"

"Mom," I said softly, "It's not just what he saw...it's what he felt...life as he once knew it was over for him, Ma!" My eyes began to brim with tears, I felt a tightening in my throat and I continued with the hope my mother wouldn't think I went off the deep end. She'd seen me go through so many phases in my lifetime. "Mom, I saw them too...they showed me the most incredible sights...things are happening to me Mom...I, uh, I touched a kid who had just got run down by a car...he was bleeding Ma...I touched him, he opened his eyes and the bleeding stopped... Something's going on, Mom..."

"What are you two whispering about?" Dad interjected, "Jillian giving you trouble?"

"No Dad, we're good," I fibbed, "Just talking about your crazy brother-in-law!"

"Truthfully, John, he had me wondering...thought it was going to happen in his lifetime, apparently it didn't!"

"What was going to happen in his lifetime?" I questioned.

"Oh, I'm not quite sure I understood what he was talking about... something about an encounter between extra-terrestrials and earthlings... that for the first time since Adam there was going to be peace on Earth... Nice thoughts, I guess...but your uncle didn't live to see it."

Mom grabbed me by the shoulder, kissed me on the cheek and said, "You'd better get home to your wife...she's not feeling good...go ahead, thanks for your help...and be careful driving. We'll talk tomorrow!"

"Go on; get outta here," Dad joined in, "Thanks for coming...say hi to Jill and the kids!"

I kissed my Mom and Dad goodnight and headed past their driveway out to the street. I gave one last wave as they slowly shut their front door, and then reached out my arm to click the remote to open the drivers' side door. Before stepping into my car, I stopped and looked heavenward. Out in the distance, a bright light hovered over the rooftops of the old neigh-borhood. At first glance, my heart skipped a beat and I got the uncomfort-able feeling I was being stalked from the skies. On closer look, however, I convinced myself it was only a helicopter that was combing the area trying to track down an escaped convict or local reprobate. Strangely, at the moment, I found that thought to be much more comforting. I started up my car and headed towards the parkway for the long ride home. For the entire drive, my head was swimming with thoughts of Uncle Pete and as to why my parents had never thought to make mention of his experience.

~STRANGE SIMILARITIES~

Life seemed to get stranger by the day. I finally learned after so many years I had an uncle who lived the later part of his life carrying around the same secrets I held. What was even more curiously odd to me was the fact my parents never told me. I spoke to my Mom the day following my Dad's birthday gathering and asked what she thought about my confession. My Mom laughed and said in a playfully understanding tone of voice, "Johnny, when you've lived to be my age and have heard all that I've heard, nothing comes as a surprise!" For a fleeting moment I wondered, "What else hasn't she told me?"

It's difficult to describe in words, but the three dimensional world I was accustomed to living in for my entire life was no longer the reality I took for granted. An awareness of another realm, another dimension, something I was unable to fully grasp, but something that had obviously grabbed hold of me, became part of my consciousness. I began to sense I was always bordering on two plains, the "hold-in-your-hand, see-with-your-eyes" physical world and the "feel-with-your-gut, see-with-your-soul" supernatural world. My greatest frustration was not being able to share the sensation with my friends and family because, understandably, they would have thought I was insane.

One Saturday afternoon, not long after my parents had enlightened me about my Uncle Pete, I was sitting idly in my backyard basking in the sunlight. There was nothing I enjoyed more than to feel the tranquil warmth of the sun encircle me, enabling me to drift off into a dreamlike state, free from distractions and the cares of this world. As I slowly sunk deeper and deeper into my mid-day trance, images of my friend Ross began to swirl about in my mind. I could see him laughing, singing, and playing his guitar. I could have sworn I almost heard him speaking to me. Startled by how real his presence seemed, I snapped out of my twilight stupor, shook my head and wondered how and why that had happened. I figured, what better time to give him a call than right when I was thinking about him. I reached for the phone and dialed. Before the phone even rang, I heard Ross's voice, "Hello...John?"

Initially puzzled, I asked, "Ross?"

"Hey man, I didn't even hear the phone ring!" he laughed, "I was dialing you!"

"What are you talking about, I just dialed you...holy shit," I said, "This is too fucking coincidental, calling each other at the exact same second!"

Ross laughed again, responding as if it didn't surprise him, "Yeah man, this kind of shit has been happening to me a lot..."

I told him how he suddenly came to mind as I was drifting off to sleep and I was overcome by the strongest compulsion to call. He had a similar explanation as to why he called me.

"Last night I had this outrageous dream about one of the songs you wrote being played all over the radio," he spoke in his raspy voice, "It was so fuckin' real and all I could think about was getting to a phone to call you. I was so bummed out when I realized it was only a dream. Since I woke up this morning I haven't been able to get that tune out of my head and I've been strumming it on my guitar all day. Then it was like something just made me reach for the phone and call you. There's some crazy shit going on, man!"

"I know what you mean, Ross. Lately life has been taking on some very unusual turns for me too. I'm trying to figure it out and I'm sure there's got to be a reason we're on each other's minds!"

We were chatting for a while when Ross brought up the time we last saw each other not too long ago. "Hey man, we never did a get a chance to talk since Melinda's wake…You think Jeffrey lost it that night or what?"

"It was a great performance," I said half jokingly, "I don't know for sure if anybody knew what to think! What happened to everybody? We're all getting old and peculiar! Remember when life was simple?"

"Yeah, man! I know what you mean…."

"How have you been? You sound a little frazzled…" I asked, hoping I could get some clues as to why we've been on each others' minds.

"Something's been going on with me, man, and I'm thinking maybe we can get together soon to shoot the shit one night. I've been feeling like I'm carrying this weight around and I can't seem to shake the premonition the world's in for some kind of rude awakening…"

Ross and I agreed to meet for a beer the following Friday night at a local bar not far from his apartment. I couldn't wait.

For as long as I've known Ross, he was not a man of many words. He would usually process his thoughts carefully before verbalizing them. Never one to jump to conclusions, Ross would listen, absorb, then nod his head slightly, look down and say, "Yeah, man!" Trying to get an opinion or a judgment from him was like pulling teeth. On that Friday night, Ross's words flowed.

We met at Flynn's Tavern, a neighborhood dive where our band used to play in the late 70's. Unlike us, the place hadn't changed an iota. There was still a phone booth, with a working pay phone, no less, standing just inside the entrance of the joint. The once white ceiling was yellow from the years of cigarette smoke that clouded the room. The bottom half of the walls were just as I remembered them…heavily shellacked oak-stained tongue and grooved pine boards. The upper half was still covered in the same non-descript off-white, blue-striped wallpaper, which was curled up and peeling at all the edges. Hanging proudly on the wall behind where the band used to set up were the same Ballantine and Tuborg Gold neon signs, beers that had become as extinct as dinosaurs. Back then, Flynn's had twelve beers on tap, more than any other bar in a fifty mile radius. That's the one thing that had changed. With the exception of Guinness and Sam Adams, all beer was available only in bottles. From what we were told, Tim Flynn, the original owner, was still kicking at 97 years old. He still owned the place but let his grandkids manage it. A small piece of our past wasn't quite ready to let go. Flynn's was still hanging in there, sort of like Ross and me.

Ross and I sat down at a small table towards the rear of the bar and toasted our long friendship by tapping together our overflowing steins of Guinness. There were a fair amount of laugh lines branching out from the corners of his blue-green eyes, but his skin was smooth and unblemished. He still had a youthful look about him in spite of a hairline that had insisted upon inching backwards. He wore his hair in the same unkempt style, pushed straight back hanging several inches over his collar. "So, where do we begin?" Ross asked with a curious grin on his face, "I think this is going to be a long night!"

I figured I'd start at the beginning, so the first thing I explained to Ross was how after dabbling in different belief systems in search of some deeper truth, I had somewhat of a "spiritual awakening" and totally severed all ties with religion. I told him about the evening when I had a dream-like encounter with some Divine entity, totally freeing me of guilt, superstition and any of the emotional baggage that had seeped into my consciousness through indoctrination. I spelled out how rough it had been not being able to see eye to eye with Jillian on spiritual matters. While Ross leaned back, sipped on his beer and listened attentively, I sensed no sign of disapproval. My story then segued into what occurred on the night of December tenth.

"Ross, if you don't think I'm crazy by now, what I'm about to tell you may just do it!" I said smiling.

Ross coughed to clear his throat and in his hoarse yet gentle voice replied, "John my friend, nothing is going to top what I'm going to tell you!"

During the next few hours, the two of us shared our similarly fascinating stories, so not a word spoken by either of us came as shocking or implausible.

"You've known me a long time," Ross spoke in a tone more serious than I'd ever heard him speak, "I'd never been a religious guy and haven't set foot in a church ever since I was thirteen. When I heard through the grapevine you were into that Born Again shit, I thought you had lost your fuckin' mind…"

"Yeah, well that was a moment of temporary insanity…" I interrupted.

Ross laughed, and then continued. "I was just shocked, man; I never thought you'd fall for that stuff…and by no means am I a fuckin' atheist or anything. I have to believe something's definitely out there…Life just didn't happen. People call it God, but whoever or whatever God is, religion hasn't got a fuckin' thing to do with it…it's all manipulative bullshit, man, it's all fear-driven!"

Ross gulped down the last few ounces of his stout, took a deep breath to try and regain his composure, and then proceeded. "John, I don't quite understand what's going on. I don't know if I should be at peace or scared to death. It can't be by chance you and I just happened to be thinking about each other at the same time and have similar stories to tell. I mean, there's got to be a reason…it's got to make some sort of sense. I saw some amazing shit, and the fact you claim to have seen the same shit…well, at least I know that I'm not crazy!"

"Unless we're both crazy," I said jokingly! I told Ross all about the light in the sky, the way time seemed to stand still, and the amazing visions of past, present and future. I told him how I'd been feeling like I was teetering between two worlds and how I felt the ever-present certainty that something momentous would occur in the not too distant future. Because I thought it may have been a little too much for Ross to handle, for the time being I decided it might be best not to disclose the story involving the kid on the bike and the way he seemed to be miraculously healed by the touch of my hand.

"I know what I saw that night, Ross…and I would bet my life it was a UFO…but how and why would beings from other worlds be able to reveal so much…unless they'd been observing us for eons…and more so, why me? Why you? I don't think I'm all too comfortable in learning that we've been under the scrutiny of extraterrestrials and human life on planet Earth is nothing more than an experiment from space…I feel like I'm playing a freakin' role in a science fiction film…"

"Listen man," Ross cut in enthusiastically, "That's why I kind of think me and you are sitting here right now. You always seemed to be more into the religious stuff than I was, or at least you have a much deeper understanding of it. I, on the other hand, was always more of a science head. You know how I've always loved exploring the possibilities that UFO's were for real. You can't tell me that Earth is the only planet in the universe with intelligent life…if you want to call humans intelligent!"

"Yeah, so what are you getting at?" I asked.

"John, maybe there is a correlation between science and religion. You're probably the only person I know who's not going to look at me as if I were crazy when I tell you what's been happening to me. I can't believe I'm even sitting here about to say what I'm going to say…"

Ross stood up, reached for my glass, shook his head and said, "We're gonna need a few more of these," and then strolled up to the bar for a couple of refills. For a few minutes, I sat alone at the table waiting for him to return and for a brief moment, I wished I was living somebody else's life. A sudden wave of overwhelming wonderment took hold of me when I saw a rather attractive woman walk from her barstool to an old fashioned juke box located on the wall adjacent to where we were sitting. She seemed to appear out of nowhere and was dressed like an old hippie, donning in faded jeans, sandals, matching turquoise necklace, bracelet and earrings and an off-white India cotton blouse. "We need a little music in here, don't you think?" she called out and then placed a few quarters into the slot. It was just too coincidentally fitting for the situation at hand that the first song she selected was "Spirit in the Sky" by Norman Greenbaum. "Bet you haven't heard this one in a long time," she said as she looked directly at me and winked. I answered her with a smile and as "Spirit in the Sky" played in the background, Ross returned with two overflowing refills. He placed my beer down in front of me, took a gulp of his, and then plopped himself down into his chair. Suddenly realizing what song he had been unconsciously listening to, he said, "You hear that shit?" I turned around, about to point out to Ross the lady who aptly chose to play that song, but she wasn't anywhere in sight.

"What's wrong?" Ross asked.

"Nothing, man, nothing," I answered, "Just imagining something, I guess…"

Grabbing onto the table, he pulled himself a little closer, took a deep breath and laughed just before saying, "Okay my friend, are you ready for this?"

I leaned over, put my elbows on the table, rested my chin on my clenched fists and said, "Let me have it!"

Ross spoke. "At first I thought I was losing my mind," he confessed like a kid in a confessional. "For my entire life I'd always been somewhat of a UFO enthusiast. I loved to talk about space and flying saucers convinced that they had to exist, and yet I have never even seen one. I've watched every documentary, every TV show on anything that had to do with that shit! At the same time, anyone who'd ever approached me about issues of faith and believing in their God, I wanted nothing to do with; I don't think I've said a prayer since grade school! This is why I felt led to talk to you, man! I felt like I saw something…not a vision, not a dream…I fucking saw something…and no matter how hard I try to explain it or describe it…unless somebody sees it for himself, there ain't no fuckin' words that can do it…"

The intensity in Ross's voice was gripping to say the least. There was no denying he really saw something. As to what he actually saw, he was hoping I had a viable explanation.

"John," Ross continued in a softer tone, suddenly mindful that he may have been talking too loud, "One night I was lying in bed. I was having a hard time falling asleep while thinking about Mom, who's been pretty sick. You know, the thought of losing her and all…just tossing and turning trying to make sense of things. Then, from out of the blue, this blinding light came beaming through my skylight and the entire room was glowing. Initially, I didn't know what to make of it and I was fuckin' terrified. For a minute I thought it could have been a helicopter, but I heard no engine noise. My brain was scrambling trying to come up with a rational explanation, but the brightness kept getting more and more intense. I wanted to leap out from my bed, but I felt paralyzed. I panicked as soon as I realized I couldn't move my legs, but then, instead of fighting it, something extraordinarily reassuring persuaded me to surrender. It was not until I did, when I felt this incredible peace. I was remarkably calm as I perceived myself drifting. I know this is going to sound like I'm insane, but it was like I vaporized…like I was one with the light and everything around me. Then suddenly, it was just as if movie scenes were rapidly playing through my mind. Images were flashing through my head quicker than I could grasp them. It was like someone or something was feeding me consecrated information; like the mysteries of the universe were meant to be revealed to me. Even though everything was happening at such an intense speed, not allowing an image to remain with me long enough for it to sink in, two of those images would not leave my head…"

Anxiously anticipating what Ross was going to say next, I could feel my heart race as I motioned for him to pause. "Hang on a second, man, I'm getting the shakes," I said while taking a couple of deep breaths. "Okay," I cued him to continue, "Give it to me slowly!"

"I'm never going to forget it, John…it was so damned real. You and I were sitting on top of a mountain…we were way up there, like right up with the clouds. We were looking down; all we could see was black smoke rising, and from within its center, continuous flashes of exceptionally bright light. You turned to me as if you were going to say something crucial, your mouth was moving but I couldn't make out anything you were saying. The more I mentioned I wasn't able to understand you, the faster and faster you spoke, until your words were formless, as elusive as a howling wind. Then as instantly as the image came, it went."

"Geez," I gasped, "That was pretty intense; would have scared the shit out of me! I'm afraid to ask you what else you saw."

Ross took no time to answer.

"The other scene forever stuck in my mind is that of a beautiful girl. She was Asian and couldn't have been too old, maybe twenty, twenty-five. She was sitting on a rock in the middle of a large body of water and all she seemed to do was cry. She appeared to be so burdened by sadness and I tried calling out to her, but she couldn't hear me. The more she cried, the higher the water rose around her. Frantically, I tried every which way I could to get her attention and when we finally made eye contact, she vanished. She didn't just disappear, she gradually minimized; shrinking faster by the second, until all that remained of her was a teardrop. Then the teardrop just seemed to evaporate. She was gone, and then everything, including the lights, faded away. Before I could even attempt to reason what had just happened, the movement came back to my legs. I didn't know if it was all a dream, in fact, I didn't know what the fuck to make of it. For a second, I even considered it might have been a flashback from the acid I took thirty years ago!"

"Why didn't you tell me any of this when I saw you at the wake," I asked. "Even then I had a suspicion there was something going on with you."

"Up to that point, John, I didn't know what to think. I didn't know if I was going crazy, I wasn't sure if it was all something I had imagined. It wasn't until what happened just recently, when I realized something has obviously been trying to get my attention."

"There's more?" I questioned.

"I haven't told a soul about this occurrence either...but I'm telling you. Something's been watching me, guiding me; it's like I'm never alone, and to tell you the truth, thinking about it's been making me feel a bit uneasy!"

Ross repositioned himself on his chair, then leaned over and quietly went on with his story. "John," he said as if he knew he had no choice but to continue, "How long have you known me? Fuckin' almost forty years, right?"

"At least," I answered.

"Well the day before we spoke on the phone, man, the weirdest thing happened to me. I was just coming out of a deli in downtown Brooklyn, picked myself up a sandwich for lunch. I don't know what the fuck came over me, but my eyes focused on this Hispanic woman and who I thought may have been her kid. They were standing on the corner waiting to cross the street. The woman was holding the kid by the hand and I couldn't keep myself from staring at them. With no clue as to how or why, I began having such strong, yet strange feelings of attachment towards her. All of a sudden, I felt extremely vulnerable. It was like I had no control over my emotions as I was surprisingly overcome with this impending sense of gloom. I was trying like hell to shake it off, when suddenly I started feeling this intense heat in my body emanating from the very center of my gut. Man, it was like nothing I'd ever experienced before. I thought I might have been getting a fuckin' stroke, and then, as if something uncontrollable took complete charge of me, I ran over to the woman, gripped her and the child by the arm and dragged them, against their will, away from the corner and closer to the storefront. The woman began to scream and punch me anywhere she could land her fist and all I could say was 'Please move away…Please move away,' and in that split second, this car sped wildly out of control, jumped the curb and crashed right into the very corner where the woman was standing. They would have been fuckin' killed and it was as if I knew it was going to happen…"

I'd never known Ross to be a highly emotional guy, and in that rare moment I saw his walls come crashing down. He bit down on his bottom lip, turned his head and then took a long deep breath. "Every time I think about it, I relive it…" he said shuddering.

"After escaping what could have very well been their deaths, the woman wouldn't stop clinging to me. She was trembling and talking a mile a minute in both English and Spanish…I couldn't understand anything she was saying except for 'Gracias.' Next thing I knew, the police showed up, people were pointing at me, the cops were questioning me and I had no idea as to what the hell was going on, except to suspect that something supernatural had been moving me about like a fuckin' chess piece!"

I told Ross all about the ordeal I went through with Brian, the kid on the bicycle, and some of the other unexplainable events that had recently entered my life. He paused, he laughed and then he said, "You know, if anybody else were telling me these stories, I'd think they were nuts, and here we are with these bizarre inexplicable tales and who the fuck is going to believe us?" Once again, Ross asked the unanswerable…"Why you and why me?"

"One of these days, this is all gonna make some sense," I said optimistically.

Ross, looking exhausted, pushed his empty glass to the center of the table and conceded, "That's it for me, man, got to drive home…"

I agreed, we both stood up and made our way towards the tavern's exit. As I pulled open the door leading to the street, a woman's voice called out, "Have a good life, gentlemen!" Ross and I turned around as we exited the bar to find ourselves face to face with the same juke box woman I was unable to locate earlier. "You do the same," I replied a bit taken by surprise. She smiled, gave us the two-fingered peace sign and then disappeared into the night.

"Where did she come from?" Ross asked.

"No idea, Ross, I have no idea!"

Ross shrugged his shoulders, chuckled and said, "I'm ready for anything!"

We shook hands, gave each other a supportive hug and agreed to stay in touch. The sky was clear, the stars were sparkling. I gazed up and laughed. "Something up there's definitely trying to tell us something, man!"

~NO NEWS IS GOOD NEWS~

For quite some time previous to the sighting and the effect it had on my life, I had become what I considered an "In the Moment" kind of person. I didn't see the sense in looking back to the past or in worrying about the future. I tried as best as I could to take life day by day. In some respects, I guess retirement afforded me the luxury to live that way. I had a decent pension check showing up every month. I was by no means living the lifestyles of the rich and famous, but I was making ends "almost" meet. Every now and then it used to occur to me how life was nothing more than the struggle to acquire the legal tender to go on living. Food, shelter, clothing and transportation all required money and as the years rolled along, the amount of money needed to simply survive increased dramatically. I was never really sure how, but we'd always seem to manage. Even though money never became a major concern, my "Live in the Now" personality was being taxed and it had nothing to do with paying bills. I had become inarguably preoccupied with when and where I would have the next encounter with that someone or something. I was becoming impatient about knowing what was ultimately going to happen, and worried about possibly losing my mind before it did. Even though I was very well aware all I had to do was trust that the powers that be would allow everything to work out as intended, I became maniacally absorbed with my role in wanting to change the world by waking people up. I also became a little concerned over the slight possibility my obsessive overenthusiastic mindset might eventually exclude me from the plan. I knew I had to relearn how to relax, be attentive, and allow things to just take their course.

Life as I had known it, especially as a young man, was most definitely not the same. The things I once took for granted were gradually fading from the picture. Since I was a kid, the population of the planet had grown astronomically. Things were heating up practically everywhere around the globe and as far as I could see, the world was just like a pressure cooker about to blow. The environment, the economy, the gap between political parties and religious denominations worsened daily. A couple of close friends of mine had lost their jobs, along with their future funds, finding themselves in very stressful and scary situations. At a time when they were counting on retiring, they were forced to take on any menial job to help put food on the table. Too many of us had become so accustomed to having life's finer things, we were spending the money we didn't have as if the supply was inexhaustible. Credit had become the bottomless means for instant gratification. People were loving things more than people. Mankind had become prisoner to rituals, traditions, and to the little worlds we had all created for ourselves. We took our eyes off the big picture, that is, caring for each other and the planet. Not that the Earth's survival was ever dependent on us taking care of it. We have always, and will always, need it more than it needs us. The Earth did fine before humans were here and it will do fine once they're gone. I couldn't stop thinking about how it might not be long until that thought became a reality. It certainly didn't appear to me the fate of civilization was looking good.

As much as I was opposed to watching broadcast news, Jillian felt the need to be informed on a 24 hour basis. The television was always on, another factor creating the chasm between us. Some nights I would just surrender, plop down on the couch and allow the negativity oozing from the TV set to bombard me. "This is not healthy for us," I would comment, "Why fill our heads with all this depressing information…there's nothing we can do about it, so why sit here and get sick over it?"

"You can't hide your head in the sand," she would reply, "You ought to be aware as to what's going on in the world!"

I would sit there and think to myself, "Oh, if only she knew…"

It was always the same old news: murder, war, terrorist attacks, environmental and economic disasters, sex scandals and racial unrest. In my heart, I felt deeply saddened over how the condition of the planet had greatly deteriorated during my lifetime. It was also discouraging to realize how history hadn't taught us anything. What was it that motivated men so much they thought nothing of brutalizing each other and ravaging the very earth that sustained life? Time was running out and only a handful of us had a clue. But then again, was it all just part of a Divine Plan?

When the news was over, the local stations would broadcast reruns of old situation comedies. We must have seen the same "Seinfeld" episodes at least a thousand times, yet we sat there almost every night in a practically vegetative state, until we dozed off. Why we just never retired for the night and went to bed, who knows? For quite a few years, as far as I was concerned, watching television had become mind-numbing and a complete waste of time. On this one particular night, however, I started getting fidgety, so before conking out on the couch, I got up to go the kitchen to explore the cabinets with the hopes of finding some healthy snack food. Just before leaving the den, I heard these sobering words come blaring from the TV: "This is a special news bulletin from Fox News …"

(I only tolerated Fox because they aired "Seinfeld"). I made an about face and planted myself back on the sofa.

"…Al Qaeda terrorist groups have taken responsibility for the suicide bombings that have just moments ago caused massive destruction throughout many of the world's major cities…"

"Oh my God," I cried out, wanting in the worst way for what we just heard to not be real. "Here we go again," I sighed, recalling the morning I heard the news about 9/11, "They went too fuckin' far this time…"

Jillian reached over and held my hand tightly, "Those poor people, John, those poor people!"

~NOT JUST ANOTHER PRETTY FACE~

The world was all abuzz with the disturbing news of the latest terror attacks. Once again there were rumors about a military draft and full blown retaliation against the Middle East. The free world was reliving the nightmare of 9/11. People were frightened, and, not knowing where to turn, they flocked to their places of worship. There was standing room only in the churches. This time the entire world was threatened. Terrorist masterminds had successfully synchronized simultaneous bombings around the globe. World leaders were holding emergency conferences at the U.N. and the War to End All Wars was certainly brewing. As much as I was sickened about the events, I knew somewhere deep within, all the strange occurrences in my recent life were about to make sense…if knowing that even made any sense!

Jillian's church was having round the clock prayer meetings and on this one late August afternoon she felt compelled to attend. She asked me if I cared to join her, but I just couldn't see myself returning to the place I fled so many years ago. Once I crossed the bridge, so to speak, there was no turning back. I had asked her to join me for a walk on the beach and mentioned I had some important things I needed to talk to her about. I tried to gently imply that maybe the answers to the world's problems weren't concealed within the walls of a church. Her reply was, "You go worship the waves; I need to pray!"

The weather was unseasonably cool for a New York August, so I decided while Jillian was seeking comfort and praying for miracles, I would head over to the beach to try and console my saddened spirit by gazing out at the seemingly endless ocean. As I walked along the boardwalk, it was easy to tell there was something terribly amiss in the world just by the numbed looks on the faces of the passersby. It seemed as though nobody was talking or even smiling. People just traipsed along and nodded in ineffectual attempts to acknowledge and reach out to each other. I felt as if I were in a dream. Everything seemed surreal… the sound of the tide sweeping the shore, the rumble of bicycle tires on the boardwalk's planking and the distressed cries of the sea gulls. Even the birds soaring through the heavens so freely seemed to sense the impending peril.

After walking a mile or two, I took a seat on a bench that overlooked the beach. The view was spectacular. The sky was a cloudless powder blue and the sunlight waltzed upon the ripples of the unusually calm waters. I took a deep breath while trying to grasp how hatred could exist in such a beautiful world. Just then, a young woman sat beside me. She looked amazingly familiar. She let out a long gentle sigh, turned to me and said, "Quite beautiful, isn't it?"

"Aja?" I asked excitedly, although I was absolutely certain it was her.

"You remember me!" she said smiling softly.

"Of course I do…don't think I'll ever forget that night! How's your Dad?" I inquired.

"Thanks for asking, that's sweet of you," she replied, "He is fine and has put that awful night behind him…but all things do happen for a reason!"

"What brings you here, other than this magnificent day?" I questioned, even though I already knew what her answer was going to be.

"You are! As I said, all things happen for a reason. Otherwise, how is it that I knew to find you here?"

Aja did not look like she could be more than twenty-five years old but she seemed to have the insight of someone who's lived forever. She was extraordinarily beautiful. Her long, jet-black hair shimmered in the sunlight and her smile was captivating. Her eyes were penetrating and goodness seemed to radiate from her very being. Part of me wanted to be thirty years younger, but the better part of me knew Aja was no ordinary girl. I also got the impression she was about to impart a great deal of wisdom upon me.

"I'm sure you knew from that moment in the bar we would meet again…You cannot deny the connection, correct?" she asked.

"I felt quite a powerful energy coming from you that evening…I wasn't quite sure I understood, but if I told you what I, uh…"

"I know what you have been going through," she interrupted, "I am here to reinforce what you are already quite aware of. Your ability to see with spiritual eyes, beyond the false notions man keeps trying to establish as truths, has placed you among those chosen to…"

"Chosen to what," I asked a bit exuberantly, and then politely demanded an answer, "Will you reveal to me what you know?"

Aja kept her eyes on the horizon and in a tone slightly above a whisper, she began to question me. "Do you not know your own soul? We are all joined by the same spirit; only very few recognize it…You already know the answers to your questions…"

"What will happen to the others? What about Jillian and my family?" I asked, even though she was right, I did already know the answer.

"Do you need to hear from my lips what you already know? Would it make it any truer?"

"Humor me," I said smiling, "It might make it a little less painful..."

When Aja turned to face me again, her eyes sparkled and I felt as if I could see into the depths of her tender soul. For a brief moment, she had appeared to me as if she were beyond human, having supernatural qualities liken to a heavenly being. Feeling as if I had fallen under her spell, she spoke to me with words that seemed to seep into my consciousness like water soaking into desert sand. "There is only one Truth, my friend, and you acknowledge that Truth. No civilization can remain when Truth is not honored. All things apart from Truth will ultimately bring destruction...but spirit is eternal, timeless...Truth is incorruptible, yet men have continually tried to twist it to suit their needs, thus resulting in the collapse of their civilizations. Life, however, continues and civilizations will rise up only to crumble again until Truth is embraced..."

"But the sightings...what about..."

Aja continued before I could complete my thought. "The universe is infinite and every creation is an eternal part of that boundless universe... We are all the materialization of Divine Intention...to try and believe otherwise is complete foolishness...To believe that only Planet Earth supports life is also foolishness. What you have seen are those who have evolved to live in Truth. They travel the galaxies freely, like all beings, they are manifestations of the Creator...only uncorrupted...love as it was intended...They have lived amongst men for countless generations, never forcing their ways upon them, never disclosing their identities... they have guided and taught. Much of the technology of the planet is by way of their elevated consciousness...Man has chosen whether to use it beneficially or destructively...The Creator, however, knows every heart and what it longs for..."

"But…" I broke in almost impolitely, "What's the point? Why does the Creator allow evil to occur? Why not just let it end once and for all? Why have only so few awakened…Why can I feel what others cannot? What makes me any better than…"

Once again, she cut my questioning short, "Do not allow your mind to interfere with your soul. Your soul knows its purpose. The mind is afraid of the soul; it yearns to control what cannot be controlled. This I am sure you are well aware of or else this moment would not find us speaking…The mind is challenged by the things only the soul already comprehends…"

"As much as I understand, I am confused," I confessed uncomfortably, "Why should it be such a struggle, as much as I know every word you speak is honest and true, part of me resists…It fights my better judgment. It tries so hard to suffocate me with doubt…"

Aja smiled compassionately and answered, "Genuine love is allowing someone the freedom to choose…Our Creator bestowed upon us what mankind has defined as 'free will'…Everything comes down to a simple choice…We either choose to believe what has already been programmed into us, or we choose to waste countless lifetimes seeking the man-made untruths that weaken us and separate us from our eternal source…You have chosen wisely…I am your messenger…Listen to your soul."

At that moment I truly recognized more than ever before the depth of who I was. All of earthly existence and the things men have strived for became no more than illusion. I knew without reservation I was one with the Universe. I felt the powerful connection to everything around me; there were no boundaries between myself and the air, the ocean. I felt Aja's soul joined to mine and it was joyful. Yet at the same time, I felt grief for all those who could not and would not experience such blissful and harmonious pleasure.

Aja and I stood up together, and then walked the remainder of the boardwalk before parting company. She encouraged me to not let the news of this world dishearten me while she reaffirmed that all things work out for the ultimate good. She referred numerous times to Jesus as an enlightened being, an embodiment of Truth and how his profound words were so badly misinterpreted and twisted to fit the greedy agendas of man. "Jesus freely gave his life," she said, "because he knew who he truly was. He was completely aware of the worthlessness of his physical body; he understood the journey of the eternal soul within. Like the Prodigal Son, the wandering soul will inevitably return to the Source."

We spoke briefly about the many natural disasters the planet was facing. Aja's simple explanations seemed sensible.

"How do you suppose the highly advanced spacecraft you witnessed travels among the stars?" she questioned. Feeling a bit like a student who knew the answer, yet was reluctant to raise his hand for fear of being incorrect, I let her answer.

"Everything visible and invisible is energy. Energy is inexhaustible… it is at our disposal to accomplish anything. Those vehicles move about the galaxies by encapsulating the very energy that simply exists. The technology was quietly introduced to man many times over but intentionally squashed time and time again because of greed." She paused, gazed out at the ocean, sighed deeply, and then continued. "Oil is the lifeblood of Mother Earth and she is being drained of it faster than she can replenish…Mother Earth was not designed to be drilled. A good number of what they define as natural disasters are just the consequences resulting from man's careless disrespect of the planet. For as much as humanity has claimed to believe in a higher power, they have misgivings, reservations and doubt. Jesus said, 'You will perform miracles greater than these,' yet does anybody trust they can?"

I did not want my time with Aja to end. Her voice was soothing and self-assured; it seemed to put me at ease. Her words were powerful, convincing and passionate. Her very presence rejuvenated me. I knew, however, that for the time being, we would have to go our separate ways. She encouraged me to remain strong, to be led by my soul and to not allow the mind to try and figure out what only the soul understands. I watched as she walked steadily into the distance with certainty in her every step, feeling once again as if I were teetering on the line between fantasy and reality.

~CAN LEAD A HORSE TO WATER~

I think what frustrated me more than anything was Jillian's obstinate attitude toward whatever I had to say that was threatening to her belief system. As much as we no longer thought the same about the bigger issues of life, I truly loved her and wanted nothing more than to share my experiences with her. I was also painfully aware, as long as she was unwilling to at least reassess some of those religious concepts that were ingrained into her mind, it would not be long until I would have to continue my journey without her.

Every day the news of the world worsened. Unemployment was out of control. The Government was practically bankrupt. Islamic terrorist groups were brazen as suicide bombers were striking in different parts of the globe on an almost daily basis. The times appeared undoubtedly apocalyptic and Christians the world over were waiting for the triumphant second-coming of Christ while attempting to solve the ongoing mystery of "Who is the Anti-Christ?" I could not say for sure if I was following my heart or my mind, but I thought since I wasn't able to get through to my wife, perhaps I could get through to her pastor.

It was a strange feeling to be pulling into the church's parking lot. I hadn't been there in years. There was a car parked in the space reserved for the pastor, so I assumed he had to be in his office. I rang the bell and within a few seconds the pastor's voice came over the intercom, "Good afternoon, Word of God Church of Brookside, Pastor Joel speaking!" I introduced myself and at the sound of the buzzer, pushed open the door to let myself in. Displayed on the main wall of the church's vestibule were two new additions since my days as a member. One was a wooden plaque with the words, "Sinners Welcomed Here" and adjacent to that was a rather large framed poster of Jesus crashing through the clouds on huge white horse. Jesus was in his usual white flowing robes, clutching a sword in one hand and holding onto the horse's reins with the other. I found the artist's rendering of the Man of Peace to be extremely out of character.

Pastor Joel met me in the church lobby and cheerfully greeted me. We shook hands just long enough for it to feel awkward. He loosened his firm grip and I pulled away. Out of his customary and conventional three-piece suit, complementing tie and black brogues, he was comfortably dressed-down in a navy blue jogging outfit and shiny-white Nike running shoes. His salt and pepper crew cut was 'mousse-d' perfectly in place and the scent of his designer cologne filled the air around him. "Hey John, what a lovely surprise this is," he exclaimed, "What brings you here after all these years?"

I followed him back into his plush office and took a seat on a very comfortable leather sofa while he sat across from me in his matching leather recliner. "Would you care for a cup of coffee?" he asked, "just made it!"

"No thanks, Joel, I'm kind of coffee'd out for today," I answered, "Two cups in the morning's my limit!"

"So, how can I help you?" he asked with an inquisitive smirk, "Re-thinking things?"

"On the contrary," I replied rather confidently, "Actually I'm here to ask you to re-think a few things!"

"Really!" he blurted out, somewhat taken aback by my reply, "And how's that?"

"Joel, do you believe there's life on other planets, in other galaxies?"

He looked at me a bit dumbfounded, probably not expecting a question of that kind, and after pausing a few seconds, he answered diplomatically. "Well, I suppose there could be," he said carefully thinking out the remainder of his response, "It would be somewhat presumptuous of us to assume we were the only creatures in God's infinite universe!"

Joel's fingers began to nervously tap at the arms of his chair anticipating my next question. "What would you say if I told you I had an encounter with a UFO," I asked almost as if I were trying to entrap him.

"What exactly do you mean when you say 'an encounter'?" Joel responded with a little hesitation in his voice.

"I mean, I saw a UFO as plain as I see you sitting in front of me and I mean that somehow, some way, whoever 'they' are, enabled me to see the unexplainable…Joel, I saw the past, and I saw the future…"

"Now, now John…hold on a second," Joel remarked with an expression that bordered somewhere between him thinking I was either crazy or knew something secretly sacred. "You know," he continued, "The devil is always at large trying to get us to take our eyes off Jesus…What you saw could very well have been Satanic…"

"Come on!" I retorted as if he were trying to insult my intelligence, "You don't believe that for a minute. Listen to me Joel; if you had even the slightest inkling as to the extent of what I've recently experienced, you would be rethinking everything you've ever preached, everything you've ever cleaved to as Truth. The revelations I've been exposed to could very well be reason enough for me to tear down the steeple and put you out of business or for you to have me burned at the stake…"

"What's your point?" he cried out annoyingly, "Why are you telling me this? What do you expect me to say?"

"Joel, I didn't come here to argue, I simply wanted to give you something to contemplate. Didn't you ever consider that maybe you're wrong, that maybe Christianity is one huge hoax?"

"I'm secure in my faith," he cried out assertively, yet not believably.

"In all honesty Joel, let's tell it like it is. Don't you think you've got yourself a pretty good gig here?"

"What?" he replied in a tone that let me know I was getting under his skin, "Are you referring to doing the Lord's work as a good gig?"

"And what exactly is the Lord's work?" I asked a tad sarcastically, "Keeping people from seeking their very souls? Keeping their egos fed by making them believe theirs' is the "One True Faith?" Instilling in them the false hope they're all going to be raptured? Reinforcing the myth a devil is lurking about causing all the evil in the world? Come on, Joel… You can't sit there and tell me you honestly believe all that, can you?"

"John, believe what you want to believe, but the words I preach bring comfort…What's so wrong in…"

"Truth lies within every soul, Joel, not in the pages of a book! Why keep people from the Truth they deserve…Didn't Jesus say the Kingdom is within?"

"Why do you quote from a book you don't believe is the Truth?" Joel asked as if it were a trick question.

"Listen Joel, the reason I'm here is because I know, as sure as I know you're not about to give up your cushiony job, that something immensely huge is about to shake up this planet and I don't mean the second-coming! I don't know how, why, when or where, but whatever it is, I want Jillian to be at my side…As long as she keeps swallowing the bullshit you preach at her…"

At that moment I heard my own words echoing in my head and I realized they weren't coming from my soul. I was agitated and somehow I let my mind kick in and take over. I knew there was nothing either Joel or I could say that would influence what Jillian believed. "I'm sorry Joel," I repented, "I'm out of line. Jillian can choose for herself; after all, free will has to account for something." I stood up and reached out to once again shake the pastor's hand. He rose, extended his hand and said what seemed to me was heartfelt, "Follow your soul, John, follow your soul!" as if he knew I was on to something.

~LIKE FATHER LIKE SON~

When I was in my rebellious youth, I can remember being politically involved. The nation's young people seemed to have a sense of camaraderie as we took to the streets to put an end to what was a senseless war in Southeast Asia. In my mind, all war happened to be senseless. Music used to have a sense of morality, so to speak. Songwriters wrote passionately about love and peace. Just like his Dad, Daniel was a devoted musician. He lived and breathed rock and roll and wanted nothing more than to support himself by means of his extraordinary talent. I made it a point to have frequent conversations with him about the hardships of trying to make a living in the music business, while being discerning enough not to discourage him. What I found rather disheartening, however, was how Dan and most of his comrades didn't seem to give a rat's ass as to what was happening in the world. Maybe that was a good thing; I wasn't sure, but somebody had to try to influence the masses. Ignorance may be bliss, but eventually, heads must come out of the sand and face what's going on. How would there ever be a shift in consciousness, if somebody didn't lead the sheep? Then again, did Jesus really influence what had become of this civilization? As powerful and deep as his words truly were, if they even were his words, man used them as a method to divide and conquer.

Likewise, John Lennon's inspiring songs of love, peace and karma were hijacked by corporations, used in advertising campaigns and practically turned into fashion statements. Most of the religions that have sprouted up in Jesus' name were judgmental organizations claiming their way was the only way, amounting to quite a few "only ways." Over twenty-thousand sects of Christianity had managed to materialize throughout the world, each with their very own variation on a theme.

Daniel's musical ability secured him the drummer's seat in several touring bands, which helped him to keep his head just above water financially. He was on the road often, so whenever he happened to be home, I used those opportunities to try to get into his head, to get a grasp on what he thought about. One rare evening while he was hanging out in his room strumming on one of my guitars, trying to figure out the chords to a John Lennon tune, I knocked on his door.

"Come on in...Hey Dad, what's up?" he asked casually.

"Not much and too much," I answered, hoping to get some dialogue going, "Miss not having you around so much these days..."

"Hey Dad, where do your fingers go for an 'A suspended 4th?"

I reached around him and directed his fingers to the appropriate frets and strings. "Here you go..."

"That's it?" he said somewhat pleasantly surprised, "That's an easy one!"

"Lennon was amazing, wasn't he?"

"Yeah, he sure was," Dan agreed, "He was a freakin' genius!"

"Talk about influencing a generation..." I added, "Wouldn't you think with everything going on in the world today, by now, a new voice would have risen up from your cohorts to try to awaken people...Nobody seems to give a shit...Unless of course the "powers that be" want it that way?"

"What are you talking about, Dad, the 'powers that be?'" knowing my fondness for conspiracy theories.

"Haven't you been paying the least bit attention? Things aren't too good, you know?"

"Dad, I'm twenty-three years old...I've got my whole life ahead of me. I don't want to think about that shit...it's depressing."

"Dan, I don't want to bring you down...but just take a look around. Maybe they don't want people to wake up...maybe that's the plan...just maybe they don't want another John Lennon coming along...I mean you've got to open your eyes...The fuckin' world's probably in the worst shape it's ever been in...Every fuckin' country, including our own, has nuclear weapons facing each other, extremists are blowing things up all over the place...and nobody's doing anything to try and change it! What happens if they reinstate the draft? Don't you ever give a thought to this stuff? Don't you wonder about what's going to become of everything? Don't you ever wonder if a God or higher intelligence plays a part in all this?"

"Dad, I'm not sure about anything...If you want to know the truth, nothing makes any fuckin' sense. Religion's all bullshit...Just look what it did to you and Mom and to me and Johanna! Dad, you're miserable... You can't even express your thoughts to Mom without an argument. Mom claims she prays for you, Johanna claims she keeps praying for me...What a waste of time! Praying for what? So we can think like them?"

Dan gently placed my guitar onto his bed, stood up, then started to pack some of his clothes into a small suitcase. I sensed his frustration and asked, "Another road trip?"

"Yeah, I'm doing a mini-tour with 'The Penetrators'...they're paying me pretty good. I'll be home in two weeks."

"You know what amazes me," I asked.

"What, Dad? I know you're gonna tell me even if I don't want to know!"

"That people are going to shows in spite of the world situation…"

"What do you want people to do, Dad, sit home and mope…Can't change whatever's gonna happen…life goes on…"

"For how long, Dan," I sighed, "for how long?"

Dan let out a deep sigh, ran his fingers through his brown shaggy hair, scratched his straggly beard and when he answered me, I realized that his journey was his own. He had to figure things out for himself, the same way I did. "Dad, you lived your life…I've got my own road to travel…It took you over fifty years to think the way you do now…Let me have my time…I'll figure it out."

In a way, I knew he was right, yet I also knew he wasn't going to have fifty years. I wasn't quite sure just how receptive he would've been if I began to tell him about my newfound theories on UFO's, life on other galaxies and his eternal soul, so I didn't. I hugged him tighter than I think I ever had before and I felt my throat tense up. "I love you Dan, but please promise you'll do me a favor…"

"What, Dad?"

"Don't stop seeking…The answers will come if you really mean business!"

"Don't worry, Dad, I'll be okay…"

~OBLA DI OBLA DA...LIFE GOES ON~

Even with imminent disaster looming over everyone's heads, life went on as usual. People were more opinionated than ever. They still argued over politics and pointed fingers at each other, as if it were opposing political preferences that caused the mess we were in. Most folks had no clue that politics was nothing more than a game of leap frog, Democrats and Republicans taking turns at four years in the hot seat. I found it maddening and extremely difficult to believe the majority of Americans could not see past the facade. Somewhere hidden in the pages of our country's history, a few devious, ingenious masterminds conceived a plan that would ultimately make them obscenely wealthy. The plan was simple but brilliant, distract the masses and divide the population, using two major ingredients, politics and religion. History had proven time and time again, "A house divided cannot stand." Obviously, it worked like a charm. The government supposedly, "...by the people and for the people," was a concept that had long faded into oblivion. I used to get nauseous whenever I heard Americans wrongfully boast about their country being founded on Godly principles because I always assumed God was opposed to murder, rape, greed and deceit. To most of my friends and family, I was just an eccentric rebel whose ideas were as far out as the ET's I was beginning to believe were coming to my rescue.

The sinking economy eventually had an effect on my household. Not only did Jillian get laid off from her job of twenty years, but the band's agent called to inform us a couple of the clubs we played at regularly were closing down. The cost of living had gotten further and further out of control and the condition of America's backbone, the working middle class, had deteriorated rapidly to what could be considered poverty level. Even the bare necessities had become unattainable for large numbers of people. Households had grown increasingly larger, as extended family members and friends had to share living expenses. Never had I expected to see what I once thought was the wealthiest and most resilient country on the planet turned upside down. It had become almost as if the working class became the slaves of the political elite, laboring for them instead of vice versa. If taxes got to be any higher, citizens just might have been ordered to sign over their paychecks.

As I realized the world was coming apart at the seams, I learned to trust my soul. I understood what most people mistook for reality was merely illusion. Just because something was invisible to the naked eye did not necessarily mean it wasn't there. I reasoned that my encounters with Aja and Ross were meant to be, because like them, I had always been keen to the idea that what we lived and experienced in the physical world could not possibly account for everything. There were countless religions that flourished upon the Earth, all of them burdening their followers with rules and conditions. Adhering to those laws and doctrines brought with it the hope of an eternal life far beyond what their earthly one had to offer. The biggest mistake every earthly civilization has made throughout the ages was, as the song said, "looking for love in all the wrong places..." The keys to Heaven, Utopia, Nirvana, Eternal Joy, or whatever and however men have cared to describe it, resided within. The soul of every man had always and will always hold the Truth…the soul is Truth, Truth is Love, a fragment of the eternal light alive in every creature. The secret is to hold on to what was with us before birth, then carry and rely on it throughout our lives.

After my enlightening discussion with Aja, what dawned on me ever so clearly was the undeniable truth of the immensity of the eternal Universe. Living life in a world that seemed to only understand scarcity, a world governed by the concept of supply and demand, my new awareness of unlimited surplus had set my spirit soaring. Why hadn't earthlings ever learned to conquer the fear of insufficiency? The proof had always been all around us. The abundance of creation should have struck humanity as humbling, but instead man hoarded and became greedy. Men became prisoners of their minds by not choosing to seek the freedom of their souls.

I knew it was only a matter of time before I got the call informing me that the Open-Mic hosted by my band was coming to an end. The owner of the club cried the blues about no longer being able to afford what he originally agreed to pay us. I was kind of bummed out over it because playing with The Cocktails was a pleasant diversion to the recent craziness in my life. Live music had become a rarity due to the so many venues closing down. The owners of the few clubs that remained open only featured bands that would play for drinks. I had to break the bad news to all the Open-Mic regulars that all good things eventually come to an end and the one who took it the worst was Vinnie.

It was on a weekday afternoon when I decided to drop the bomb on Vinnie. He lived for those weekly jam sessions. Reluctantly, I dialed his number.

"Hey Vinnie," I said rather upbeat, not trying to distress him with any somber inflections, "What's going on?"

"Nothing much, Johnny," Vinnie replied, sounding happy to hear my voice, "What's up?"

Bad news was always preceded by questions like, "What's going on?", "What's happening?" and "What's up." Vinnie went through a pretty bad divorce several years ago and his life had been reduced to a two-bedroom, third floor walk-up in a not-so-desirable neighborhood. He'd been collecting social security disability, put on more weight than he ever dreamed possible, and the only escape from his mundane existence was getting out and playing the blues with us every week.

"Vinnie, I've got a little bad news for you," I said gently...

"Fuck," Vinnie moaned, "I don't want to hear any fuckin' bad news! I hear enough fuckin' bad news on the radio and the TV every day... What the..."

"Hey Vinnie, get a grip, it's not that bad," I assured him, although I knew he wouldn't think so.

"Alright, fuckin' tell me already, don't give me a fuckin' anxiety attack..."

"They cancelled the Open-Mic..."

There was silence...

"Vinnie...Vinnie," I repeated, "Vinnie are you there, man?"

After a long deafening pause, Vinnie continued, "Sorry man, I got a touch of killer heartburn," he said apologetically while letting out a colossal belch. Then without missing a beat, he let loose. "Are you fuckin' kidding me? Why? Why would they do something as idiotic as that?" he hollered, "That fuckin' place doesn't know a good thing...Motherfucker! I love playing with you guys, now what the fuck am I gonna do?"

"Vinnie," I called out, raising my voice just enough to be heard over his ranting, "When business picks up they'll bring us back...things are rough out there, man..."

Vinnie whimpered, "That's all I look forward to, Johnny...I'm so fuckin' pissed off right now you have..."

There was another very long silent pause. "Vinnie, Vinnie are you there?" I shouted into the phone.

There was no reply. I could hear the faint sound of gasping and then a sickly thud. At first I didn't know if he was just toying with me, but after a minute or so I realized something was wrong. I immediately called 911 and made a mad dash over to Vinnie's apartment. On the ride over I was thinking the worst. He hadn't been in the best physical shape for as long as I'd known him. He seemed to grow larger every week and never even considered cutting back on the beer and fried calamari. After performing his three songs with the band, he would breathe heavily and sweat profusely, as if he had just run a five mile marathon. He was truly a walking time bomb.

Overcome by my own zeal, my thoughts once again turned to the kid on the bike who was hit by the car. I thought, God forbid anything tragic had happened to Vinnie, the powers that be could work through me and produce another "miracle." I arrived just after the ambulance got there. A policeman met me at the front door. "Are you a friend of his?" he inquired.

"Yeah," I answered despondently, "I was the one who made the call...we were in the middle of a conversation when he, uh, passed out, I guess..."

The distraught look on my face, combined with some polite coaxing, persuaded the officer to allow me to enter the apartment, but I could see I was too late. Vinnie was already onto the next phase of his soul's journey. There was his hugely overweight body lying face down on his bedroom floor with his cell phone clutched in his right hand and a crushed acoustic guitar under him. Blood was oozing from his head, so he obviously hit it on the one piece of furniture in the room as he descended. When I saw Vinnie lying there motionless, surrounded by police and EMT's, as heartbreaking as it was for me, the sensation just wasn't there. There was no stirring in my gut, no heat, and no uncontrolled reaction. I realized it wasn't up to me. It was Vinnie's time.

"Was he agitated?" the officer interrogated, snatching my attention back to the matter at hand, a large dead body in the room.

"A little upset I imagine…" and I explained to the officer what probably riled Vinnie enough to what the medics said had set off a massive heart attack.

After the EMT's placed Vinnie's body into the ambulance, the police asked me to step back into the apartment as they needed to ask a few more questions. They wanted some contact information on family members or friends. I was no help to them because the only relative Vinnie had ever mentioned to me was the ex-wife he hadn't spoken to in years. Somehow, I had the sad feeling The Cocktails were his only friends. When I looked around at the squalor Vinnie had been living in, it depressed me terribly. I noticed his familiar Fender Stratocaster leaning against his unmade bed alongside a stack of library books. I picked up a few of the books and noted they were all overdue. They were taken out on the eleventh of December, the day after Mick and I confided in Vinnie about "flying saucers," and strangely enough the subject of every book involved UFO sightings. He never once mentioned them to either of us.

Although it was sad, Vinnie had always been an accident waiting to happen, so when I had called the other members of The Cocktails to tell them the sorry news, as much as they were grieved, they weren't surprised. With Open-Mic getting cancelled, the probability was very slim we were ever going to see Vinnie again. On that day, the probability became a certainty, at least in this world.

When I pulled away from Vinnie's apartment, I took a deep breath, wiped the few tears that snuck out from the corners of my eyes and by force of habit, turned on the radio. The song coming from my speakers, even though it wasn't one of my favorites, could not have been more appropriate, "... Obladi, oblada, life goes on bra, Lala how the life goes on..."

~WHEN IT RAINS, IT POURS~

I'd always heard my grandmother use the expression, "A watched pot never boils." I finally figured out what she probably meant by that… Live your life and everything will happen when it's supposed to happen. At least that's what I wanted it to mean. Waking up every morning and wondering, "Is today going to be the day?" was getting a tad unnerving, especially since I wasn't exactly sure of what I was waiting for.

After a slight tease of possible peace negotiations regarding the war-torn Middle East about a year ago, the world had backslid once again and became volatile due to the numerous amounts of reoccurring violent acts attributed to Islam terrorist groups. Fundamentalist Christian groups were making reckless speculations as to the identity of the so-called Anti-Christ. It almost seemed as though they thrived on disaster and global doom just to bolster their insane beliefs. They longed for the return of Jesus so desperately, it didn't matter what devastation the world would have to confront. There was one popular televangelist from Texas who actually organized a gathering of over five-thousand of his followers for a "Bring on the Nukes" revival meeting. His twisted way of thinking was, the quicker the bombs drop, the quicker the Lord would appear in the clouds.

Although at one time there had been talk of a draft, because of the crippled economy and the lack of jobs, the number of men and women enlisting had become greater than any time in American history. This ensured that the reinstating of a draft probably would not happen. News of that made Dan kind of happy. He had already alerted me to the fact, come the chance he'd have to don a military uniform, he'd be over the border in a heartbeat. Shiploads of America's youth were bound once again for the waters surrounding the planet's trouble spot and Dan and I were ecstatic he was not among them. A call from Chuck conveyed the news he was not as happy.

"What was I going to do, John, I tried to convince him otherwise, but he didn't want to listen. He went and fuckin' enlisted and we just got the news he's shipping out in two weeks," Chuck reported practically in tears.

"There's nothing you can do, Chuck, Bobby's an adult…he's got his own road to follow," I spoke firmly but sympathetically, "Besides my friend, you know yourself it's only a matter of time…"

"A matter of time for what, I don't know if I'm following you, dude?"

"When we talked, Chuck, you certainly sounded convinced it was only a matter of time before our space friends made contact…"

"Why can't they see it, Johnny…Why doesn't anyone fuckin' see it? If people just realized we weren't alone, maybe we'd get over ourselves and there wouldn't be any more fuckin' wars!"

"Eventually everyone's gonna see it, Chuck, you don't need me to tell you that…"

"I know bro," Chuck sighed, "I know, it's just that he's my son, man, I don't want to see my son get blown to bits in a god-damned desert!"

Chuck and I continued our conversation for a while. It was somewhat distressing for me to hear my friend speak so exuberantly about the idea of visitors from other worlds finally making their grand appearance on

Earth without any connection to anything spiritual. As much as I wanted to confide in Chuck about my exploits with Ross and Aja, connecting with strangers, feeling uncontainable compassion and a restlessness in relation to something extraordinary about to go down, I knew I couldn't. I didn't think he would get it. His soul wasn't ready and his mind was still too connected to the illusion of the physical world. He told me how difficult it had been going to work every day knowing how his son chose to shake hands with the devil by joining the military, particularly in such apocalyptic times. We agreed we would try to meet within the month, provided we had a month.

Meanwhile, life had taken a sudden twist in the lives of Jillian and me. My brother Mark had called to announce the unexpected news of our Dad having been rushed to the emergency room. It appeared as though he may have had a stroke. At that moment, I couldn't believe it. Although Pop was 87, he seemed the picture of health. I knew the next few days were going to find me travelling back and forth to the hospital and giving my Mom some moral support. I had to consider myself lucky that both my parents had remained relatively healthy most of their lives. When the numbers started creeping into the high eighties, calls, such as the one I received from my brother, were certainly to be expected.

Not even a few hours after Mark's devastating phone call, I got the bad news from Arizona. In spite of Jillian's blunt disapproval, her folks had retired to a suburb of Phoenix in what seemed like lifetimes ago. The last time I saw Jillian's Dad was about ten years ago at her Mom's funeral. My mother-in-law had lost a battle with cancer which took quite a toll on Jillian at the time. My father-in-law, an ex-New York City cop who got accustomed to the climate, decided to remain in desert country rather than burden any of his three kids with his idiosyncrasies and obstinate behavior. It was unfortunate, but from the day I met him, our relationship was strained to say the least. Political and religious differences had really built a wall between us. Neither one of us had been able to keep our opinions to ourselves.

Jillian had only two siblings, older brothers who she also hadn't seen in years. Jeffrey was a gay, unattached, semi-retired, unmotivated hairdresser, who had moved in with his Dad a few years after the Mom died and always seemed to be broke. Why he was never able to find Mr. Right could possibly be attributed to the fact he hated to work. He'd get hired at a salon, work six months, build a following, then call in sick and never show up again. He was a unique individual. Knowing my father-in-law's religious standpoint, it must have killed him to have had a son who was blatantly homosexual.

Eddie was the oldest sibling. He was a divorced, childless, semi-successful entertainment lawyer living in Anaheim, California. For as long as I'd known him, he's made claims of rubbing elbows with several high-powered show-biz personalities. For years he'd been promising me he would get my demos in the right hands. I figured he never found the right hands.

"Hey John, it's Jeff…Is Jillian home?"

"Hey, Jeff, how's it going?" I replied cautiously, knowing his calls usually meant he either needed a favor or there was bad news to report. "No, she's not," I continued, "She'll be back in an hour or so…." In spite of his boldness in asking to borrow money or his eagerness to announce gloom, I'd always liked Jeff. He was very open-minded and easy to talk to, so unlike his sister and father.

"Where'd she go?" Jeff asked in that effeminate tone unmistakably his.

"Where do you think, Jeff? Where does she always go…?"

"Oh! Don't tell me she's at church again!" he groaned.

"You got it my friend…she's praising the Lord!"

"Jesus Christ!" he retorted, "Haven't you gotten through to her yet?"

"I'm afraid not, Jeffy boy, I'm afraid not…Hey, I know you didn't call to talk about your sister's church habits…what's up?"

"I think she's going to have to fly out here. Dad's in the hospital. They're not really sure what's wrong yet…Couldn't catch his breath last night. They got him all hooked up with wires and IV's. Eddie's taking a flight out tomorrow."

"Was he sick or anything, Jeff?" I asked obviously concerned.

"He's almost ninety, John; something's bound to go wrong sooner or later…can't live forever!"

In my mind I thought, "Ah! But we do live forever!" but figured it would be wisest to keep those thoughts to myself.

"I'll have Jill call you when she gets in," I assured him, "Talk to you later!"

When Jillian got home from her prayer meeting, I told her to call Jeff immediately and gave her the report about her Dad. Needless to say, the news disturbed her, not entirely because her Dad had taken ill, but because traveling to Arizona would be a major inconvenience.

"Shit," she said, "The last thing I want to do is to fly out there now, especially not knowing how serious it is." Although her words sounded somewhat callous, I knew Jill didn't have the best relationship with her Dad. Ever since he moved out West, they spoke to each other less and less. After her Mom died, I could have counted on my fingers the amount of times Jill and her Dad conversed. Jill took it personally when he made what she called the selfish decision to settle out west. She liked having her Mom nearby and never forgave him for taking her away from her and our children. It really was kind of sad and extremely hypocritical for two headstrong Christians to have held resentment towards one another, especially father and daughter.

"I'll call him in the morning," Jill said while slamming the closet door, "I don't feel like dealing with this right now..."

"Not for nothing, Jill," I commented, "You just left a prayer meeting at church...I don't get it, where's the compassion, the forgiveness...He's your father for God's sake!"

"That's right!" You don't get it," Jill snapped, "Your father didn't run away from his grandchildren. Mine has never been there for us and now I'm supposed to drop everything and run to his side. My brothers never call me unless there's a problem; let them deal with it for now!"

"What if he dies?" I asked, "You're going to eat those words...You'll never forgive yourself...Jill, he's your father!"

"I told you, I'll deal with it in the morning, I'm going to bed!" she repeated, and made her way upstairs.

"By the way," I called out as she was half-way up the staircase, "Speaking of my father, Mark also called tonight. My Dad's been hospitalized...I'm heading over there in the morning..."

"What happened, is he okay?" she asked, with more concern for him than her own Dad.

"I'll find out tomorrow...He said they think he might have had a stroke."

Upon hearing the news, Jill made an about-face, sped down the stairs and put her arms around me. "What's going on?" she sobbed, "This really sucks..."

The following morning Jill called her brother and discovered the prognosis wasn't good. Her Dad contracted a severe case of pneumonia and because of his age, the doctors didn't seem to think he was going to pull through. Jillian was obviously upset over the sudden realization her Dad could die, and even more upset over the fact that I couldn't take the trip with her. She hated to fly alone, but she knew I had to stay behind to contend with my Dad. Samantha, however, agreed to disrupt her busy schedule and accompany her mother to Arizona. Thank goodness we had a ton of credit card miles available to pay for the airfare. Jill was able to book a flight for later that very morning and within a harried couple of hours, the three of us showered, packed, and drove to JFK where airport security was tighter than ever.

I didn't know what hit me, but as I left my wife and my daughter at the gate, I became suddenly overwhelmed by the disconcerting possibility I may never see them again. My eyes teemed with tears and Jill asked, "Are you alright?"

I was momentarily swept away by thoughts of how much of our lives together we wasted by clinging to our egocentric attitudes and opinions, holding grudges, and forsaking our souls over the foolish illusions of right and wrong. I took a deep breath and answered, "Yeah, I guess I'm just a little overcome by everything…I'm going to miss you!" At the same moment, the very concept of time became an unreality.

"Oh Daddy," Samantha remarked, "We're not going to be away forever!"

"Be sure to tell your Dad I'm praying for him," Jill requested.

"I will and for what it's worth, tell your Dad I love him and send my best!"

I took Jillian in my arms and held her tight. I was annoyed at myself for all the times I didn't practice what I preached by getting myself entangled in senseless arguments and speaking unkindly. The words "I love you" flowed from my lips in a way I hadn't felt in a long time… deep, passionate and genuine. I presumed because life had thrown us some sudden curve balls, I realized how we had been taking each other for granted. Jill told me she loved me, kissed me goodbye one last time as our impatient daughter moaned in disgust, "You guys are nauseating… let's go before we miss the plane!"

I stood behind and waved goodbye until they were out of sight, feeling weighed down by an unexplainable sadness. I trudged my way back to the car and then made the dreaded trip over to the hospital to see what was up with my Dad.

Observing my Dad lying in a hospital bed all wired up to beeping and flashing medical devices was crushingly upsetting. I could not recall his being sick even once. When I arrived, my Mom and my sister Diane were already there. The pale green walls along with the faded beige curtains separating my Dad's side of the room from his wheezing roommate's added to the dismal atmosphere of the room. Mom looked fatigued as she and Diane stood alongside his bed, both of them staring lovingly into his distant eyes. My Mom had always been young at heart, so she never looked her age. That afternoon, however, I saw a frail, old woman standing before me, agonizing over the stark reality she could be losing her life companion. The lines of age around her eyes and mouth, which I rarely ever noticed, were greatly accentuated. Diane looked up and acknowledged my presence with a weary nod. I leaned over to kiss my visibly heartbroken sister, then without moving her eyes from Dad, my Mom reached out her arm towards me. As soon as our fingers met, she clutched my hand with whatever strength she had, giving no indication she would ever let go. I was pretty sure my Dad had no idea as to who was even in the room. Every few minutes his eyes opened wide and he gazed directly up at the ceiling as if something were trying to get his attention. In my mind, I envisioned myself laying hands upon him, seeing him sit up and saying, "Get these wires off of me and get me the hell out of here." Unlike the results with Brian, the bicycle boy, I had no impulse anything of that nature would be reoccurring. It was confusing and frustrating for me to know how, beyond the shadow of a doubt, higher forces had worked through me once before and had yet to return in times of need. At the scene of Vinnie's death and there at my Dad's bedside, either the supernatural forces had left me stranded, or I had failed to realize they were always there.

Two nurses entered the room and kindly asked us to wait outside for a few minutes while they checked my Dad's vitals. As we walked along the corridor to a small lounge at the far end of the floor, I glanced into several of the rooms and saw in bed after bed, medical science at work trying desperately to prolong life. As much as I didn't want my Dad or any other of the patients I passed to die, I was absolutely confident, that even after the shrill monotone beeping of the flat line on the monitor screens, life continued in the invisible realm. In my spirit, I knew for certain, each of us was on our own eternal journey. Just like the flowers and the plants that withered away and died every fall, only to rise up again in the spring, so too, we return…again and again. Signs of rebirth and indications of perpetuity were all around us, yet we somehow ignored them and opted for finality and gloom. Once more, I kept my thoughts to myself, sensitive enough to know the depressing hallway of a hospital was neither the time nor place.

Mom and I were still attached by our hands. "He was fine, it was so sudden…" Mom whispered.

"He's in good care, Mom, Dad's tough, he's gonna be alright!" I replied, trying to lift her spirits.

"How's Jill and the kids?" she asked, genuinely concerned.

"Well, I wasn't going to say, but since you asked…" and I went on to tell her all about Jill's Dad taking ill and her unplanned trip with Sam out to Arizona.

"Oh my goodness," Mom quivered, "You should be with your wife…"

"She'll be okay, Mom, she's with Samantha and if she should need me for anything, I'll get a flight out there…At the moment, I need to be here with you and Dad."

"John," Mom softly called my name while squeezing my hand, "Whatever happens to Dad, I know he's going to be just fine. He's a good man."

My mother never seemed to verbalize her point of view about religion, the hereafter and the like. She just went along with the program, following along in the traditions of my Dad and the generation before her, but she never appeared too committed. Somehow I knew there was a lot more going on in her heart and mind than she let on. Although completely perceptive that life was too mysterious and way beyond our capabilities to figure out, she chose to keep those thoughts private.

Diane didn't say much that afternoon; my Dad's sudden condition seemed to devastate her. "Maybe we should go back," she suggested, "He's going to wonder where we went." I didn't have the heart to tell her, Dad didn't even have the faintest idea where he was, never mind our whereabouts. "How fragile and uncertain man is," I thought to myself as we made our way back to my father's room, "One day you're as feisty and sharp as ever, the next, you're reduced to a helpless, speechless sack of flesh."

"Theresa and Mark should be here soon," Diane mumbled, as if that could change the situation. Within the hour, my two other siblings arrived to help with the monotonous tasks of watching and waiting. It was a long grueling day, filled with lengthy pauses, forlorn gazes, cell phone calls from nieces, nephews and grandchildren, small talk and no change for the better in my Dad's worsening condition. Moments before visiting hours were over, a priest entered the room and announced he was there to administer what Catholics referred to as "Last Rites."

Mom looked at me tenderly, and reading my mind she said, "Dad's still Catholic, he would want it this way." It wasn't a time for opinions.

We all made our way down to the hospital lobby that evening sharing the same unspoken thought, "would that be the last time we saw Dad alive?" We bid our farewells in the parking lot where Theresa volunteered to stay with Mom, and then we all headed off in different directions, certainly symbolic of our lives. I couldn't tell if it was my imagination working overtime, but as I circled around the block to head towards the expressway, I could have sworn I saw the lights throughout the entire hospital flicker, momentarily dim, and then go bright again.

I'd lived in Lakeside for so long, I could have driven home blindfolded. That evening, as I turned left onto Elm Lane, everything was suddenly unfamiliar to me. I wasn't even sure if I had turned onto the right street. All I was able to think about was the concept of "forever." Images of my dad and Jill's dad floated about in my mind and I felt an absolute assuredness they were going to be okay; in fact, I knew in my heart of hearts, that ultimately everyone from the beginning of time has been okay. People had always been and will always be just like actors, the same folks just playing different roles, the same souls in different bodies and situations. In what I deemed as a moment of brilliance, it all made sense. Every interaction among the role-playing was intended to assist in finding the path back to our beginnings. I felt an inner-light radiate within me, not too different from the way it did on the night of December 10th.

Lena and Mr. Gambaro had just put out their trash for the next morning's pick up and waved to me as I turned into my driveway. I hesitated before returning the neighborly wave, because for a second, they appeared to me as mere observers, strangers watching me drift somewhere between the reality of eternity and the fantasy of suburban life.

"John, is everything okay?" Lena called out as she sensed my distracted behavior.

The stark sound of her voice immediately brought everything back into focus, grounding me as if I had just come down off of a mild hallucinogenic. My neighbors were once again recognizable and I clumsily replied, "Uh, yeah, Lena...Uh, I mean, no, not really...Jill's out west; her Dad got taken ill..."

"Oh, I'm-a so sorry," Mr. Gambaro joined in with his heavy Italian accent, "Tell-a Jill I'm-a ask-a fuh huh."

"Thanks guys, I will...I got to get inside to make some calls," I said politely, before hastily dragging my garbage to the curb and then escaping into my empty house.

I made two phone calls without delay. First I called Dan, who was somewhere in the country on tour with one band or another; I could no longer keep track. I caught up with him while he was on the road in Illinois and alerted him to the state of both his grandfathers. I told him his Mom was in Arizona, asked him to make it a point to call her regularly and assured him that I would keep him updated. Dan was evidently upset, but we both realized his rushing home would serve no purpose. I told him I loved him, warned him to be careful and said that I would see him when I see him. The second call was to Jillian. It was three hours earlier in Arizona so I knew I'd find her awake.

"Hey Jill," I spoke softly, as if I were trying not to wake someone, "How's it going?"

"It could be better," she quivered, "We don't think he's going to make it, he can hardly breathe, John...Jeffrey is totally freaking out...it's a good thing Sam came along...she's a good distraction for him. How's your Dad doing?"

"Things aren't looking too good over here either, Babe, it was an aneurysm that caused Dad's stroke. He's so out of it, he has no idea what's going on. I can't believe this is fuckin' happening…"

"I know you're upset, but you don't have to curse," she gently reprimanded.

"Sorry, everything's been just a bit overwhelming," I moaned, knowing she didn't have the foggiest clue as to the strange events in my life.

"We'll get through this like we've gotten through everything else," Jill said unconvincingly, "It's late there, get some sleep…talk to you tomorrow…oh, were you able to contact Dan?"

"Yeah," I reported, "Dan's fine. He's going to call you. I love you… talk tomorrow."

"I love you too; tell your Mom that she and your Dad are in my prayers. Good night."

I was extremely tired from what was an excruciatingly stressful day, yet as much as I tried, I couldn't fall sleep. The sound of Jill's voice saying "good night" replayed over and over again in my head. All the times we would get on each others' nerves, wishing for opportunities to be apart and there I was missing her terribly. I tossed and turned, yearning for the secure feeling of having her warm body nestled beside me. I hated myself for every stupid argument we'd ever had, for the hurtful things I'd said to her through the years, yet at the same time, I realized they were the roles we had to play. Every scene had to unfold exactly the way it did, for with every line of dialogue, for every burst of laughter, for every pang of heartache, there was a lesson learned.

****

~PART TWO~

****

~SHOW TIME~

If ever there was a time I was extremely certain of the constant struggle between mind and soul, it was that night as I lay in bed, totally exhausted yet unable to close my eyes and fall asleep. As my spirit seemed to be directing my attention to the desires of the collective soul, my mind was working overtime in trying to convince me it was all unproven nonsense, figments of my fertile imagination. Demanding me to stop entertaining thoughts about the supernatural, my mind insisted upon creating mental lists of all the things I needed to do on the following day; call Jillian, call my Mom, see my Dad, gas up the car, change the strings on my guitar and pay the bills. My soul, on the other hand, was alerting me to pay strict attention; the time was fast approaching for that extraordinary something I'd been waiting to occur. The mind needed to be in control while the soul could just "be."

Between the restlessness stirring in my gut and the onslaught of thoughts darting through my mind, I couldn't sleep. I moseyed my way to the kitchen, was unsuccessful in finding something appealing to eat, so I poured myself a snifter of Maker's Mark, figuring that would help to anesthetize me. It didn't.

Drink in hand, I strolled over to the den, plopped myself down onto the couch, grabbed hold of the remote and very out of the ordinary for me, turned on the television set. Quickly clicking through the late-night infomercials and daytime talk-show reruns, I settled for the local news station. The past couple of days had been such a whirlwind with the failing health of our Dads that I hadn't had a second to catch up on world events. I guess in an odd sort of way that was a good thing; the negative forces in the news had been overbearing and I had enough to deal with. In the wee hours of that morning it was no different. As a meteorologist, much too perky for that hour, excitedly tracked a hurricane headed for the northeast, words the world had been dreading for decades, interrupted the weather report. With a startled look in his eyes, the weatherman, reading from his teleprompter sadly announced, "…Missiles fell upon the city of Tel Aviv…the number of fatalities is unknown at the moment… details to follow as we bring you a special news bulletin…." I knew that was the signal alerting the world to prepare for the beginning of the end.

While reporters tried their best to inform their viewers with whatever little information they had, the continuous news loop at the bottom of my screen posting the same distressing information had me mesmerized. Just then, the sudden sound of buzzing emanating from my coffee table startled me. I quickly resolved it was my cell phone vibrating to alert me a text message had arrived. Curious as to who would have been calling me at that hour, I checked the message. It was from Ross and it simply read, "R U Up?"

I knew what Ross was going to say even before I dialed, but I dialed anyway.

"Hey man, just got your text…I guess you can't sleep either?" I asked idiotically.

"John, I'm glad you're up, man! I gather you heard what's going on…"

"Yeah, I'm just sitting here glued to the idiot box. I should've never turned it on. It's been a bad enough day with my Dad."

"What happened?" Ross asked considerably concerned. He had always admired my father based on the few times they've met.

"Sorry I didn't get a chance to call and let you know…he had a pretty bad stroke."

"You're shittin' me," Ross groaned, "He was in great shape, I thought?"

"Surprised us all," I uttered, "Doesn't look like he's gonna make it, but quite honestly, it doesn't look like anybody's gonna make it at this point! How's your Mom?"

"She's still in the home and has no fuckin' idea what's going on, which I think is a blessing," Ross regretfully admitted. "Listen, man," he went on to say quickly changing the subject, "I think I need to be somewhere… something's been gnawing at me all night. My insides have been trembling, I'm fidgety as hell and I'm getting the feeling like something's been trying to direct me to go somewhere…It's like I know for sure I've got to get the hell out of here yet I've got no clue where to fuckin' go…so I figured you might!"

As Ross was speaking to me, the sound coming from my television began to fade in and out until all reception was lost. All I could hear was a constant piercing whistle, like back in the days when television stations used to broadcast test patterns. The picture had turned to fuzzy black and white snow. For a second I was spooked as "Poltergeist" came to mind.

"Something crazy's going on here, man," I howled into the phone with a little panic in my voice. Before I could get another word out, I underwent an incredible arousing in my being. As clearly as I saw the one sip of bourbon left in the glass on my coffee table, in my mind I could see Aja. She was standing on the beach like on the day we talked and I could almost feel her dark penetrating eyes pulling me towards her.

"Ross," I cried out with a sense of urgency, "Get your ass over here right now!"

"What do you know, man? What's going on? Where the fuck are we going at three o'clock in the morning?" he interrogated.

"Never mind," I snapped, "Hurry!" and I shut off my phone.

After disconnecting with Ross, I ripped a sheet of lined paper from the notebook on my desk, grabbed a thin black marker and began to write:

Jillian, Samantha & Dan…

If you find this letter, my assumptions were correct.
You must have heard by now about the strange phe-
nomena that took place.
I could only imagine what people are thinking and
saying…
Please don't worry about me or any of the other folks
who are reported missing.
We are all fine…Obviously, our disappearance was
not by means of 'The Rapture' the church had been
expecting. We aren't alone in the Universe!
Jill, we haven't seen eye to eye on spiritual views, and I
would never say, 'I told you so,'
But I will say you shouldn't have dismissed so much of
what I've tried to share with you…
It was never a matter of who was right and who was
wrong…
It was about connecting with what connects us all…
soul.
The answers are within…You won't find them in

church, in preachers, in politics.

If you want to see 'God,' just look at the perfect universe surrounding you…

If you want to know God, look within and know yourself.

Everything works for the good.

Hell is a fear tactic, it does not exist.

And we will all meet again…We are eternal spiritual beings…

I think it was John Lennon who said death was just like changing cars…

When the ride was over in one, you just hopped into another.

I could never explain…but one day you will know.

Tell my Mom I love her and ask her to tell you about my Uncle Pete.

I love you all…

I wish you were here with me

Until we meet again,

John/Dad

I placed the letter on the kitchen table and thought, if I was crazy, I'd be back to tear it up before anybody read it. If I wasn't completely out of my mind, it really didn't matter. Before I had the chance to second-guess myself, Ross was at my door.

"I feel like I'm starring in a really bad science fiction movie," he confessed, "are we insane or what?"

"Well, we're about to find out," I replied, "You want a drink before we go?"

I poured Ross a shot of bourbon. He gulped it down, then quickly looked over the letter lying on my table and totally intrigued by the circumstances asked, "So where do you think we're headed?"

"Right now," I answered, "To the beach…let's get the hell out of here!"

The roads were not quite as desolate as I had imagined they would have been, as Ross and I cruised along the parkway leading to the boardwalk. He did not question my decision as to where we were headed so there was no need for me to admit I was being led purely by a hunch. As we approached the parking lot adjacent to the boardwalk, I noticed there were more cars parked there than I had expected to see. With a hurricane inching its way up the eastern seaboard, the winds were strong and the waves were intense, so I attributed the large number of people on the boardwalk as to being 'storm watchers.' The last thing I had anticipated was to see as many individuals as we did hanging out at the beach at three in the morning. At first it struck me as kind of bizarre that regular folks would actually lose sleep over getting wind-blown and wet just to watch the waves beat up the shore, but then the thought occurred to me, some of them could have been there for the very same reason we were.

Ross's long but thinning blond hair was being blown every which way and as he glanced about, he reiterated, "Tell me this isn't fuckin' wild, man…I'm tellin' you, this is either a dream or we're starring in a movie…"

The two of us walked along the splintered wooden planking, guided by the hazy moonlight, turning our heads occasionally to evade the intermittent powerful winds. I had no idea as to why we were there, except for the gut feeling some invincible force was leading me. A hooded shadowy figure was fast approaching us. When we were just steps apart, we all stopped dead in our tracks. It was Aja. Her eyes were instantly recognizable.

"I knew you would be here," she pronounced softly, yet confidently.

Ross stood beside me, his eyes wide open in astonishment, barely able to get his words out, he stammered, "You're the girl I saw in my dream…my, uh, vision, whatever it was I had…You're the girl who was on the rock crying…Holy…"

"Ross," I intruded, "This is Aja."

"This is too much," Ross exclaimed, "This is just too fuckin' much!"

Aja suggested we step down to the beach and walk along the sand. "There's nothing like feeling the spray of the ocean," she said with a giggle, "Besides, they should be here momentarily!"

"Who's going to be here momentarily?" Ross cried out, and before he could spit out his next syllable, the black sky above us cracked open with what appeared to be a massive blinding search light and it danced high-speed orbiting circles upon the water. Spiraling beams of radiant, greenish-blue, lightening-like coils pirouetted downward creating a seemingly impenetrable force field. State troopers were racing to the scene one after another, the brazen ones driving their patrol cars right onto the beach. With the news of the world being on the brink of a nuclear war, it was any wonder what they had imagined was happening.

I not only heard but felt a faint, resonant rumbling, hinting that something was definitely approaching. Aja held onto my hand and Ross, not knowing which way to look next, was right at our heels. Suddenly, a series of what seemed to be thousands of headlights broke through the sky, resembling the continuous popping of flashbulbs, only in reverse. The lights encircled the circumference of an immense craft that looked as if it were perched in midair. From where I stood, looking up at the mysterious brightness in the sky as the winds whipped my face with water and sand, it measured up to be the size of a football stadium. The lights were so dazzling, it was next to impossible to see what was going on around us. I could hear the distant sound of sirens blaring, the crashing of the waves upon the jetty and the distant cries of panic. In an abrupt, blinding, bursting of intense brightness, everything flashed, then suddenly ceased. There was silence, and then without warning, everything faded to black.

~OUT OF THIS WORLD~

It seemed like it was only the span of a split second while going from a state of unconsciousness back to consciousness. In what appeared to be no more than the blink of an eye, we went from the chaos of the blustery beach to what I could best yet poorly describe as a highly advanced, picturesque, futuristic yet naturalized development. Suspended way above us were basketball sized spheres projecting beams of light that illuminated the dreamscape below. Aja was still at my side holding onto my hand, while Ross ventured off to wander in amazement. The utter beauty surrounding us was so phenomenal I could hardly contain it all. The very air itself seemed to glisten and had the distinct sweet fragrance of citrus. An unquestionable aura of tranquility and peace overpowered me and I knew, without reservation, we were in a virtuous place. There was a significant amount of people roaming about, some were in pairs, and some were solo, but everyone seemed to be sensing the same consoling, peaceful feeling I was. What truly astounded me was the realization that the colorfully surreal garden-like grounds we were so freely wandering about were within the confines of a huge spacecraft. Meticulously placed about were incredibly beautiful fruit trees, bushes, flowers and the most interesting vegetation that flourished throughout. The colors were indescribably brighter than any I had ever seen. There were free-flowing brooks and streams situated all around us and the water was crystal clear. Aja and I hadn't said a word to each other from the moment we were beamed aboard until she tugged at my arm and said, "Shall we taste the water, it looks so refreshing?"

I smiled, and secure in knowing no harm would come to us, I answered affirmatively, "Why not!"

We darted over to the closest stream and while kneeling down cupped our hands and scooped up mouthfuls of water. The taste on my tongue was scintillating, yet its texture seemed weightless, as if no amount possible could ever be an excess. The excitement and elation in Aja's eyes was exhilarating, and I got the sneaking suspicion she'd done this before. I felt as if I were twenty again as the two of us strolled over to one of the hundreds of trees and helped ourselves to the most exotic looking fruit I'd ever seen. It was nothing like I ever remembered fruit tasting. My taste buds exploded as I tried my best to savor the flavor as the sweetest juices burst into my mouth and down my chin. Aja laughed as I tried to clean the mess from my face by wiping it on my arm. Facing me, she slowly moved forward until her body met mine. For a few seconds, she laid her head upon my chest, and then tenderly gazing up at me, she stretched until she was close enough to lick the nectar from my lips. Suddenly, the strangely exciting reality kicked in that I would not be returning to the life from which I had mysteriously vanished. Planted deep within my being were fond recollections of the family, friends and events I had left behind: seeds of memory sprouting images from past or parallel lives, close enough to induce joy, yet distant enough to shield me from sadness, regrets or remorse. I experienced the comforting awareness there was perfect order to all that was and to all that would occur. At that timeless moment we were ageless. Past and future were one with the present. Aja saw me for my soul, and I, for hers.

A soft blue tint seemed to slowly filter down from above, enveloping the entire area, as if a clear summer sky was dissolving among us. Then a voice so soothing, apparently speaking to our inner beings, gently guided each of us to two wide descending tunnel-like pathways located at the very center of that enchanting complex. Those walkways led to a main entrance of a lower level. Completely surrounding the sub-terrain of the craft were walls constructed of liquid screens. There were no seats, per se, just circular markings on the ground. Above the surrounding walls was a balcony stretching completely around the amphitheater-type area. Moving about on the balcony in an effortless manner, as if conveyor belts carried them along, were beings very similar in shape and size to humans. Their celestial glow, however, prevented us from identifying any distinguishable features.

There was no pushing or shoving. Everyone politely found his way down to one of the circular markings. As I stood within the border of my circle, I felt a stream of air rise up from under me, providing me with what was the most comfortable invisible chair, conforming to my every move. That same shade of blue gradually fell upon the entire group, making it appear as if we had melded with the surrounding space, and we all floated about contentedly in our places. All the while I had to keep reminding myself that the incredibly dreamlike Eden I was pleasurably experiencing was all taking place within an enclosed humongous space vessel of some kind. The atmosphere was serene, calming and seemingly divine.

Streams of three-dimensional images reminiscent to the ones I accredited to my first and only encounter with what my mind identified as a UFO, and which I surmised was less than a year ago, began to appear upon the screens around us. The thought occurred to me that perhaps

I'd been on board the ship before. I really had no concept of time at that point. I couldn't view the sun, the moon or the stars, so I had no idea of how many hours or days had elapsed since "the abduction," but I always felt revitalized, never tired.

I presumed we were all gathered together to learn why we were there. Absorbing information quicker than a sponge soaking up water, I clearly understood the relationship between the physical and spiritual. The manner in which I was able to understand was miraculous. Language wasn't essential; the knowledge I acquired was beyond words and seemed to be transmitted telepathically…All that is corporeal is the materialization of the spiritual… Everything visible emanates from the invisible. Glimpses of Earth's past, present and future displayed before us, as an unspoken communication explained how all of existence is energy, and the Source of all that energy is the mind of what man has referred to as "God." These were the very thoughts Aja verbalized to me during our walk on the beach.

A series of highly detailed scenes were rapidly being displayed before us, providing us with quite the history lesson. The pivotal occurrences from throughout the ages had been captured and replayed for our observation and enlightenment. What in Earth time could have amounted to billions of years was condensed to seconds. We were given a quick peek of civilizations completely beyond any of modern man's geological findings; civilizations that have risen and ultimately vanished from the Earth, leaving absolutely no traces of their existence. It appeared the human race had been given innumerable opportunities to begin again with expectations of attaining the level of Love intended for them. While very few succeeded, most had failed. We viewed how people, given the divine gift of "Choice," voluntarily chose to submit to fear, doubt, worry, stress, mistrust and all the other negative forces opposed to Love. On a planet so richly abundant with all the provisions necessary to sustain life, we watched mankind surrender to the lie of scarcity. Hunger has always been completely unwarranted. There has never been a reason for any man, woman or child to go hungry when one tiny apple seed has the potential to produce infinite fruit. In a manner similar to time-lapse photography, in accelerated motion, we beheld innumerable seeds produce boundless supplies of crop.

We were captivated by disquieting visuals depicting the immense pride and foolishness of men, witnessing how negativity has always been highly contagious and has caused the collapse of countless generations by means of jealousy, greed, possessiveness, ownership, repression, division, hatred and war. We saw how the emergence of the structures and the systems established by man to create money and wealth had always been his very downfall. False prophets and teachers continually misguided the unsuspecting masses by instilling fear along with fictitious ideas about death and the hereafter. It was reaffirmed for us that death was never something designed to be frowned upon, but to be viewed as a new beginning in the continuous saga of creation. The soul's journey has never been limited to Earth. All I saw and heard was confirmation of what I had always thought to be true.

Space vehicles such as the one we were in had made numerous visits to planet Earth throughout all of her transitions, always keeping a safe distance and never imposing the constraints that would have deprived mankind of its greatest gift, free will. The beings in our midst were like the guardians of the Universe, a species that had successfully achieved God-consciousness, tapping into the power of a Supreme Divinity, guaranteeing the survival of our species. They seemed to generate an aura of kindness and patience, and for an instant, I wondered if such beings were the ones referred to as angels in Holy Books. We were made to understand how all that was, all that is and all that will be, has existed always. The underlying theme recurring in all we saw and heard was that life and everything drawn to it, originated from spirit. Spirit always was and always will be. Every idea, every solution to every problem, every thought, every song had already been conceived. Nothing is ever new, just rediscovered.

It was transcendentally explained to us how Love is the highest form of energy and how all of creation, both tangible and intangible, are results of that Love. Life is therefore a gift and should be treated as so. Every creature has the awesome ability to procreate, as co-creators with the Divine. Love conquers all, moves mountains, and makes possible the seemingly impossible. Perfect Love heals, is nonjudgmental, is tolerant and keeps the Universe in flawless order. Attaining the highest level of Love allows oneself to love all things equally and unconditionally. Simply put, God is Love and Love ultimately prevails. Thus it was made clear to us, that as it was in the story of Noah, at this moment in eternity, we were chosen to once again replenish and guide a future civilization on what will be a new Earth. No one on board was taken against their will. Heartfelt desire and a deep yearning to know the ways of the Divine had each of us where we longed to be.

At the time of our departure, it was so plain to see, a shift in the balance between Love and its opposition was highly unlikely to occur on our planet at the rate it was going. I knew so well, man had irrefutably screwed up again and again, never learning from the mistakes of the past and never embracing the wisdom from beyond the stars. The world was so divided and so ridden with fear, it was just a matter of time before a total collapse of society would come about. There was no way I could ever go back.

~IGNORING THE MOON~

Time was no longer of any relevance. After what was quite the eye-opening presentation, virtually witnessing the rise and fall of previous walks of life, we were treated to the most spectacular journey one could ever imagine. The flow of air that had been keeping us comfortably suspended gradually subsided, allowing us to assume our standing positions while the misty blue ambiance dissipated. Once again, Aja was right by my side holding on to my arm. While roaming about, we caught up with a visibly elated Ross who was beaming with wonderment and accompanied by a younger woman who appeared to be of Hispanic descent.

"I'd like you to meet Gabriella," Ross said eagerly.

"Very nice meeting you," Aja and I replied simultaneously, as I wondered how the two managed to immediately connect.

Gabriella's jade green eyes shimmered behind her cappuccino complexion, reminding me of the way cactus complimented desert sand. Her long, wavy, black hair, pulled back in a loose-fitting ponytail, revealed her high cheek bones and classic beauty. With my poor ability to estimate, I would have guessed she couldn't have been a day over thirty, but I knew better than to ask a woman her age.

Ross, who I had always known to think things out before he spoke, directed his attention to me for a second, and while smiling from ear to ear, said, "Is this fuckin' incredible or what? Gabriella is the woman I told you about…She's the one who I pulled out from the path of that rampant car in Brooklyn…What were the chances we'd ever meet again?"

"Wow," I remarked a little taken aback, "Kind of like being predestined, wouldn't you say?" finding it a bit odd how a specific past event materialized so clearly in Ross' present consciousness.

"Timing is everything," Gabriella broke in smiling, "Isn't life amazing?"

She looked me over closely and said eagerly, "I feel as if I know you, as if we've been with each other before…"

I shook my head, smiled, shrugged my shoulders and said, "Could be, nothing surprises me anymore!"

Totally attentive to trying to remember where and when she knew me from, Gabriella cried, "Damn, you just look so familiar, I know I know you from somewhere. Maybe we met in a dream or in a past life…but either way, I'm sure one day it'll come to me."

Seeming to recall the details of the incident so lucidly, Ross diverted Gabriella's attempt to trigger her memory when he questioned, "But what about the child you were with?"

"He wasn't mine," she explained to Ross, "I was the child's nanny. We were out for a walk and thank Heaven you allowed yourself to follow your instincts… "

Gabriella turned her attention to Aja and commented as if she were in on a secret, "All things happen for a reason, don't they Aja?"

Before she could get a response, the flooring beneath us began to slowly slide open, making us realize that we were standing upon a sheet of crystal-clear glass plating. In the same manner as when peering out through a glass-bottom boat, gazing down, we had a birds' eye view of the galaxies. At what was an undecipherable speed, we zoomed past uncountable stars, as the starlight appeared to bounce off the craft and streak back out into the deep navy heavens. Like breathless kids riding the high-speed twists and turns of daredevil amusement park roller coasters, we shrieked with wondrous amazement as the vehicle dipped and dived among dazzling showers of glittering light. I was mesmerized by the sheer vastness of the heavens, baffled by how any living creature, specifically man, could not be humbled by the very thought of it.

Basic human logic imparts just how insignificant man really is compared to the infinite, yet it's his own prideful ego that has been responsible for his repeated self-destruction. It was evident we were among beings with a much superior intelligence and a union with the Divine. I thought about what I was taught in church, that is, with God, all things work for the good. In my core being, I was certainly aware the world I came from would be no more, but I was also confident that I would once again connect with the loved ones I left behind. Every soul has innumerable journeys and every journey is a step and a lesson learned on the return path home to our Divine Source. My purpose was to be exactly where I was. I understood that true freedom, happiness, joy and strength can only be reached by accepting the reality that each of us is a microcosm in the orchestration of the universe. Refuting it only begets weakness, frustration and dysfunction.

Ross, Gabriella, Aja and I freely roved about acknowledging the many ecstatic faces among us. We all had a common overpowering sense of brotherhood as we greeted one another with loving embraces and handshakes. Sharing with each other the similar, spiritually-centered experiences we had back on Earth before our galactic exodus, we expressed our gratitude to be on such an amazing excursion. The exhibition of planets, moons, and suns strategically placed throughout the far stretches of infinite galaxies was a sight way beyond what any of us could ever have imagined. From the very moment Divine Omnipotence allowed matter to burst upon the scene, all things magnificently took form and have been obedient in remaining in place since. Beholding all that glorious beauty carried me back to how often the moon screamed out for man's attention, just to remind him there was perfect order to all and to worry was foolishness. Distracted by ego and self-interest, lives had been spent ignoring the moon.

It was impossible not to notice how a pairing of souls appeared to be taking place. There was no logical explanation as to why I became so attached to Aja or Ross to Gabriella; it just seemed to happen, as if we were predestined. The feelings I had for Aja were like nothing I'd ever known before. Although I felt genuine love for her and was very much aware of her affection for me, jealousy, insecurity or the need to possess her exclusively, were non-existent. We had truly become one in spirit.

At that point, I could not say for sure if it was a result of the fruits we were eating, the water we were drinking or the air we were breathing, but I was experiencing an intense connection to everyone and everything around me. It was as if we all shared the same breath and had the same blood coursing through our veins. The sensation was liberating, peaceful and exciting at the same time. Several more of the celestial-like beings appeared on the scene, emitting what I could only describe as the essence of pure Love. They were like angelic tour guides, reassuring each and every one of us as to our significance in the Divine plan. Their presence alone was overpowering, reaffirming my trust that Love was indeed unconquerable. My desire was to communicate with them, to fully understand their place in the cycles of creation. I could not keep my wants hidden; they were able to perceive my inner most thoughts. As gentle as the touch of a butterfly, one who I could only define as a space angel, placed a hand upon me. Instantaneously, the phenomenon I had encountered when I laid hands upon the boy on the bike was recreated within me. I felt the heat radiate from the very center of my being, filling me with an extreme love and appreciation for all of life. The beings in our midst were the manifestation of virtuous, unadulterated Love. They were highly evolved creatures way above and beyond the narcissistic, overemotional behavior that perpetuated the ever puzzling human drama. Resultant from the intensity of a tender tap, my brief curiosity was satisfied and I completely understood the healing power of compassion.

All of our needs, which weren't many, were looked after. We were provided with nourishment, facilities to bathe, linens in which to wrap ourselves and areas to rest. Nobody was quite sure where we were headed or when the next transformation would take place, but we were all totally trusting, being fully compliant to our calling.

~HOME AWAY FROM HOME~

Our journey through the heavens was an educational seminar, where we were given first hand information pertaining to the workings of the Universe. The energy of Love was the glue, the key element holding it all together. Everything in existence was a product of that energy, from the tiniest grain of sand to the rings surrounding Saturn…from the softness of a newborn's breath to the rumbling of a volcano…from the chirping of a canary to the deafening explosion of a nuclear missile, from the pedaling of a toddler on his tricycle in the park, to the lightning speed maneuvers of the very spacecraft we were aboard. Encapsulating Love, the very essence of all matter, seen and unseen, provides the necessary power that enables the suns to give light, man to have life and superior beings to navigate freely among the stars. Earthlings had never learned to tap directly into the unconstrained power supply of the Source, even though time and time again, they were offered assistance from higher life forms. Instead, they chose to seek endless alternatives to what was always the simplest solution. Those alternatives repeatedly brought about their own demise.

Verbal exchange had become practically unnecessary. We had learned to communicate by means of expression and thought transference.

Reading each other's minds was actually pretty cool, because nobody had anything to hide. We were all of one mind and one spirit. Love had become the driving force within each and every one of us. The negative forces from the world we left behind, such as greed, intolerance, self-righteousness, self-pity, judgment and pride were foreign to us. Why man had continually chose corruption over striving to attain this utopian mindset was unsettling, although it may have been a necessary step on the return road to our preordained state of euphoric perfection.

Aja and I had become inseparable companions. We spent every moment together wandering about and meeting the others. We shared ideas, dreams and the unguarded intense pleasure of our physical and spiritual union. From the first time we crossed paths I sensed her candor and tremendous insight and often wondered if her soul had taken this journey before. She had way of reading me, seeming to know my unspoken thoughts.

"Don't worry," she said comfortingly, "Jillian and your children have come to reconsider all you had tried to show them. They know of your purpose and are at peace…You will see them again and they will recognize you in spirit."

"From time to time they've entered my mind," I confessed, "and in as much as I know there is no turning back, and I know this is where I belong, in my quiet moments, I struggle to reach back, wondering if there was anything more or less I could have said or done to have motivated them to even consider the ideas which ultimately led me here. They will always be part of me."

"Those thoughts will quickly pass, love, and when all Divine Intention is fulfilled, unspeakable joy is all we will know. Jillian had her own path to follow, but all paths lead to the same eventual destination. Truth will prevail, all will be one!"

Aja and I had found an inviting little spot nestled in the center of several flowering trees where we would go to when we desired alone time. Just before retreating there, we took one more glance out at limitless space and noticed several other similar spacecrafts playfully cruising among the great wide open. Once again, Aja knew my thoughts as I wondered where were we headed and when would we arrive.

"Rest your mind," she spoke reassuringly, "We are in the company of goodness and Love, and no harm can come to us. We will be where we were destined to be." My apprehensive human nature couldn't help but to kick in now and then, but Aja's words had a way of never failing to bring me peace of mind.

The sweet scent of the surrounding flowers was intoxicating. Aja put her arms around me, kissed me firmly on the mouth and in a moment of complete surrender, we were one in mind and body. The lighting about us began to gradually grow dim and for the first time since entering the craft, I became strangely tired. Before I knew it, I had drifted off to sleep.

As the body succumbs to the tranquil state of deep sleep and is fully unaware of its surroundings, the spirit breaks free to roam the boundless perimeters of a timeless realm, returning with visions and dreams. The gap between the moment of unconscious sleep and the point of re-awakening is intangible. Similar to when a coma-stricken patient regains consciousness, as far as he or she is concerned, no time has elapsed, although in actuality it may have been years. Leisurely exploring the far reaches of space, it was apparent that time was illusion. As it was stated in the Scriptures, a day is liken to a thousand years, thus I imagined a voyage through the black holes of the cosmos could have amounted to millions.

When I awoke from what felt like an extended period of hibernation, I found Aja awaking beside me. She stretched her slender arms to welcome the new moment, greeting me with a warmhearted smile and a tender gaze from her exotic eyes. Her striking beauty induced me to want to reach out and hold her, but as everything gradually came into focus, I glanced about and surprisingly discovered we were in a noticeably different environment. I quickly deduced that sometime while soundly asleep, we were mysteriously transported from our Eden-like accommodations to a land out from within the confines of the spacecraft. I jumped to my feet, not in a panic, but vaguely confused. Aja held out her hand for me to help lift her to a standing position. "This is where we are supposed to be," she said confidently, "we are home again."

The warmth of the sun on my face felt immensely comforting. We were standing upon a grassy hill and all around us were a variety of trees abundant with ripe fruit. Directly in front of us, there was a path leading to a seemingly never-ending body of water, reminiscent of the serene beaches Jillian and I used to frequent. The water was as clear and enticing as the replicated brooks and streams we encountered on board the star cruiser. Holding tightly onto my hand, Aja and I carefully made our way down the path to the shoreline. Hesitantly, we walked along the warm sand before braving the unknown temperature of the gentle waves caressing the shore. The invitingly warm water playfully stroking our feet seduced us to shed our white linens and dive in. I felt as if we were Adam and Eve in Paradise. As I stood in chest-deep water, I could see clearly below as Aja swam towards me. Her body was perfect without a blemish, and as she seductively rose up out of the water, she wrapped her arms around me and began to kiss my mouth with a passion I had long forgotten. I carried her closer to the shore where the water was only ankle-deep and the two of us made love as though we were the first man and woman, discovering pleasures beyond our imaginations.

Sitting on the beach, staring out at the horizon, noticing the shift in the position of the sun, I became fully aware of where we were, but a little unsure as to the timeframe, that is, if time was even relevant. When Aja stated we were home again, she was undoubtedly referring to planet Earth. The familiar taste of the salt water on my lips, the smell of the soil and the blossoming trees, and the pure whiteness of a passing cloud in the heavenly blue sky above, made me feel as if we were standing at the threshold of humanity, like something out of the pages of Genesis. We were most definitely about to embark upon a new journey and all I could conclude was, the civilization we hailed from was long gone.

After slipping back into the coverings that remained with us from our space travels, Aja and I adventured along the coastline, taking occasional detours into the jungle-like hills to taste the nuts, berries and plentiful fruits dangling from the interminable amount of trees. Everything around us was untainted, uncorrupted and wholesome. The Earth we returned to had completely replenished itself, restoring all its resources to their original chaste and uncontaminated state. I could only wonder how many earth years it took to accomplish the tremendous task of rebirth and for the extent of that period, where was I? Although we were privy to many of the mysteries of creation and the rise and fall of numerous civilizations, there were many things we had yet to figure out for ourselves. We were still human beings on the journey towards all-embracing fulfillment.

Similar to the way my life had changed when my eyes locked onto the light in the sky one wintry night God knows how long ago, was the time spent on my fantastic galactic journey also just a mere moment seeming like an eternity? For the stretch of time needed to peruse the galaxies and complete a crash course in the history of the Earth, I did not seem to age a second. My hair, beard and fingernails did not grow. I never felt unusually hungry or weary; it was almost as if I were in a state of suspended animation. We were living in amazing, yet enclosed quarters, so we didn't feel the radiance of the sun, the true sensation of the outdoors, or hear the crashing of an ocean. The entire experience could have been one instantaneous blast to my subconscious. Maybe we could have entered a parallel universe. Maybe everything we experienced was executed by means of holograms or maybe it was all a dream within a dream? At that very moment I wasn't too certain about anything except the Paradise on all sides of me and the company of a fascinatingly beautiful and deeply spiritual woman.

We must have walked for miles before Aja, noticing a figure in the distance, stopped, pointed and alerted me. "Look," she cried out excitedly, "Up ahead...sitting on the rocks...let's go greet them."

Gripping my hand tightly, Aja beckoned me to keep up with her as we ran along the warm untouched sand towards the only other two people in sight. When we got near enough for them to see us approaching, they waved, then headed in our direction.

"Ross!" I hollered, "My God, man, after all this, I could only hope it was you!"

"John, Aja!" he replied over-joyously, "Fancy meeting you here!"

Ross and Gabriella were also draped in their white space-travel wear and were just as happy to see us as we were to see them.

"Where is everyone? There were loads of us on that ship..." Gabriella asked while holding onto Ross's arm.

Aja, always seeming to know more than what was revealed to the rest of us, answered as if the voice of a higher intelligence was speaking through her. "Like seeds we have been scattered to the far corners of the earth...The remnant of 144,000...uprooted, gloriously chosen to carry out Divine will...for a brief season we experienced the realm of timelessness and just as the earth has been restored, we have been returned to restore civilization to the ways originally intended..."

"Man, it's like Adam and Eve all over again," Ross exclaimed in astonishment, "I sure hope we get it right this time!"

While the four of us sat upon the boulder-like rocks that stretched out into the soothing swells of what we presumed was the ocean, we trusted that the powers which took us here would protect and enable us to survive.

Knowing our thoughts, once again Aja responded wisely, "As long as Love rules our hearts, and we obey in the same manner as the plants, the stars and the planets, and we pass along that love to the following generations, we will have achieved our purpose and our souls will rise to the next level."

The sun appeared as a huge orange ball of fire suspended just above the line of the horizon. As we gazed out at what would be our first sunset together, meditating on Aja's words, we sat overcome with gratitude. To think we were intentionally selected to take on the tremendous responsibility of initiating a new Earth was as much humbling as it was overwhelming. The glowing intensity of the sun made it seem as though it was bringing the water to a bubbling boil as it leisurely sunk below the surface. Before we knew it, we were blanketed by an incalculable amount of stars lighting the beach like a ballroom dance floor. The night sky gave way to an enormously bright crescent moon, supplying all the light we needed to maneuver about safely.

In a sense, we had just lived through our first day. The sunset had established that our lives would once again be measured by intervals of time. It was a long first day and I was looking forward to falling asleep with Aja beside me. We noted our location and agreed to meet up with Ross and Gabriella just after sun-up to do some further exploring. No sooner than we bid each other good night, an intense bright light cracked through the sky directly above us. Hovering overhead were the friendly guiding lights of a spacecraft, very much like the one we were upon. The repetitive cycle of the intermittent bursts of light coming from the circumference of the ship was hypnotizing. Suddenly, as if floodgates were being pried open, flocks of winged creatures were being released from the vehicle's portholes, flying over our heads and into the trees just beyond us, while sea life swiftly descended down into the deep. Somehow, I suspected they would have arrived before us. I remember the story being told, that man appeared on the scene well after the birds of the sky, the fish of the sea and the four-legged beasts of the land. As quickly as it made its grand entrance above, the Noah's ark of outer space slipped through a slit in the star-covered blanket of night sky and vanished, leaving no trail of luminance whatsoever.

The once unnoticed silence had been instantaneously replaced by the cooing and chirping of birds, the humming and buzzing of insects and the splashing of fish arcing in and out of the water. It was apparent that all the creatures knew their place and purpose, exemplifying a living lesson for us to adhere to. No creature is above nature, we are all equal parts. Pleasantly awestricken by all we have witnessed, Aja and I, Ross and Gabriella retired for the evening.

~WORLD WITHOUT END~

We all had no doubts we were back on Earth. As to how long we were away or as to exactly where on the planet we had been placed, none of us were sure. We did, however, start recording time in the only method available to us, that is, by counting sunsets. Cell phones, watches, laptops, I-pods and all the wonderful technological advances of the world we left behind were also left behind. Ninety sunsets had passed since the day Aja and I awoke on the grassy hill. Daily meditation kept us tightly connected to our Divine Source, providing us with insight and the ability to accomplish all the necessary tasks for survival. We built the tools needed to construct shelter and gather food. So long as we remained true, choosing freely to honor Love, remaining in a state of gratitude, and recognizing we were one with all Creation, Heaven on Earth would certainly be attainable.

To say I was experiencing "culture shock" was an understatement. Leaving a world we once believed was so technologically advanced, and having to, sort of, start from scratch, was tremendously humbling and challenging. After encountering the travelers of the galaxies, it was evident how primitive we really were. Life back on Earth could have been as beautifully sophisticated and highly developed as it was for those who came to our rescue, but mankind abused technology by using it as a means to destroy and conquer, rather than for the welfare of the planet. Now it was up to us to start anew. We have witnessed the mistakes and poor choices of previous civilizations and we have seen firsthand the astounding power of Love. We were among the blessed remainder about to embark on a journey to hopefully keep Paradise thriving.

So used to the everyday luxuries such as just flipping on a light switch, running the faucet, making a phone call, or flushing a toilet, my new life was going to take some getting used to. In all honesty, it was a pleasant change not having to watch television, answer phones, or spends hours glued to a computer screen. The one thing I missed, however, was listening to music. It was going to be up to us to create our own. Encircled by such astounding splendor and an abundance of everything needed to sustain life, I was almost hoping future generations would remain as primal as the moment we were in. I knew, however, as the numbers of people on the planet increased, progress, development, innovation and improved ways of life were going to be inevitable. My deepest concern was that as humanity re-evolved, they did so with a conscience.

Aja and I met up with Ross and Gabriella sometime in the morning of the ninety-first day and greeted each other with genuine gestures of affection. The love linking the four of us was quite overpowering. We had become quite the loving family. We had set up some landmarks with stones and branches and then spent the day exploring our new Eden. The energy emanating from the plant life all around us was intense. We could actually sense the flowers and trees commune with us, enlightening us as to which varieties were edible, which were medicinal or which were to be left untouched. The insects, more colorful than any I have ever seen, went about their business, leaping from plant to plant, joyfully fulfilling their purpose. Most were on hand to assist in pollinating the flowers; others were present to unreservedly offer themselves as food for the birds and reptiles. As we found our way through acres of magnificent gardens and jungle-like terrain, we arrived at an area of open field where creatures resembling sheep, goats and horses grazed about. The animals seemed to amiably acknowledge our presence and were not the least bit startled. Unthreatened, they placidly continued to graze, obediently tending to their calling.

When we noticed the sun was beginning to lean towards its setting position, we followed our trails back to the beach in time enough to view another sunset. It was a period we liked to set aside each day for meditation and to worship and honor the Great Spirit responsible for all that exists. Ross and I surprised ourselves at how proficient we'd become at building fires. Evenings we would sit on the beach huddled around a fire to recall the pleasantries from our past lives and venture exciting stories about what we thought was lying ahead. Keenly aware of the destructive powers of religion and multiple belief systems, it was our responsibility to remember, educate and pass along our wisdom, to guarantee they would never surface again.

It was crazy to think we were confronting the strange reality of being away from what used to be home for what could have been millions of years, yet we never seemed to age a day. From where we stood, there were no traces of past societies, no wrecks, no remains, no ruins. One thing we became obviously aware of, however, was that the aging process had certainly picked up where we had left off. Our beards, our hair, our fingernails and toenails had resumed growing and through our collective ingenuity we designed razors from rocks and shells. We made use of the nectar and pulp from certain plants as shaving gel and lotions. Without the use of mirrors, we depended upon each other to assist with the hygiene and grooming. Aja grew quite fond of my beard, so I allowed her to trim it in the way she so desired. Aside from my reflection in the water, until this point, I hadn't been able to get a good look at myself.

As the last few embers of our fire crackled, Aja put her arm around my waist pulling me closer to her. She grabbed hold of my hand and tenderly placed it upon her slightly extended belly. From inside Aja's womb, I could feel the restless kicking of a new life, a joining of body and spirit, waiting to break out and greet the new world. Right then and there it dawned on me that prior to the descent along the birth canal, a newborn is in the blissful state of all-knowingness. It would become Aja's and my obligation to see to it our child never forgets.

Ross and Gabriella shared in the celebration by passing around the cups we had formed from thick leaves. Our makeshift drinking devices were filled with a wine-like, mildly intoxicating juice that came from the very plump colossal red berries Gabriella had discovered. We experienced the stimulating effects of the fruit after eating them one evening and made it a decree to indulge only at the end of the day. We drank to new beginnings as the fire's final sparks gasped their last breath and then the four of us wished each other pleasant dreams and made our way along the beach to our mutually agreed upon, designated sleeping areas.

Aja cuddled up close to me as we both stared up into a night sky crammed with shimmering stars. I became sadly aware of the difference in our ages and she sensed my sadness. "This is a joyous moment," she reminded me, "there is no space for unhappiness. Remember we are here to fulfill a purpose and to move on to the next journey…our souls are forever joined, my love."

I knew each and every time Aja spoke, she spoke Truth. I also knew in order to achieve our objective I had to die completely to the emotions of ego. It was our mission to instruct our children, leading them by example, never exposing them to jealousy, envy, possessiveness, pride or judgment.

It was our responsibility to remain connected in the purity of Love and to ensure the generations to follow would continue the pursuit.

Aja drew to my attention there would soon be others who would eventually make contact with us and be intertwined in our lives. Endless and exciting possibilities were waiting ahead anxious for us to find them. I took a deep breath and feeling secure from the warmth of Aja's body, I let out a sigh of gratitude. Just then, in rapid secession, six immense bright lights streaked across the stretch of blackness above us, mingled with the stars and vanished. Somewhere on this vast beautiful planet, others had been transported to help accomplish the awesome task of repopulating Earth. Not too far off in the distance, I could hear Ross's happy holler echo, "Woo Hoo!" Aja squeezed my hand tightly, reassuring me once again, all was right in the Universe.

~THE BEGINNING~

A graduate of Queens College with a degree in communication arts and a minor in creative writing, John Rullo has spent the last forty years composing and performing songs in rock bands in the New York metropolitan area. Retired from his day job, he now writes his unique blend of irreverent memoir and Socratic inquiry with the same inspiration he'd first found in songwriting. The father of three grown children, he lives on Long Island with his wife, Joann.

www.ingramcontent.com/pod-product-compliance
Lightning Source LLC
Chambersburg PA
CBHW070125260626
47160CB00004B/1629